〈15〉

THE GIRLS OF CANBY HALL

TO TELL THE TRUTH

EMILY CHASE

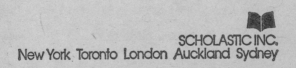

SCHOLASTIC INC.
New York Toronto London Auckland Sydney

ISBN 0-590-33759-9

12 11 10 9 8 7 6 5 4 3 2 1   8   5 6 7 8 9/8 0/9

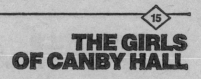

THE GIRLS
OF CANBY HALL

TO TELL
THE TRUTH

THE GIRLS OF CANBY HALL

Roommates
Our Roommate Is Missing
You're No Friend of Mine
Keeping Secrets
Summer Blues
Best Friends Forever
Four Is a Crowd
The Big Crush
Boy Trouble
Make Me a Star
With Friends like That
Who's the New Girl?
Here Come the Boys
What's a Girl To Do?
To Tell the Truth

CHAPTER ONE

You know what? I can't believe we're actually going to meet someone from Alison's family," Shelley Hyde said as she ran a comb through her curly blonde hair. She was standing in front of the mirror in Room 407, the room she shared in Baker House dorm with Faith Thompson and Dana Morrison.

"Why?" Faith looked amused as she turned the pages of a photography textbook. "Can't you believe that Alison has relatives? Did you think she hatched from a *test tube*, for heaven's sake?"

Shelley blushed, as she always did when her roommates teased her about her naive enthusiasms. "That's not it, and you know it. I just never expected — well, you know — Alison's cousin to show up here, at Canby Hall."

"Well, I think it's exciting," Dana Morrison

said, applying one last coat of polish to her fingernails. "Alison's a neat lady, and the best housemother in all of Canby Hall . . . so it's about time we meet someone from her family. And we ought to get a move on up to The Penthouse, by the way. It's almost seven, and Alison told everyone to be there on the dot."

"In that case, you'd better hope they're not holding a surprise beauty contest, girl," Faith told Dana. "Because you'll have to go in that awful sweatsuit. You can't change into anything decent, with your polish still wet."

"Oh, you're right. Ugh. I'll have to pretend it's Halloween, and go dressed as a bag lady." Dana flashed a smile that showed gleaming white, even teeth. She was a beautiful girl, tall and slim, with long, dark hair. Because her mother was a New York City department store fashion buyer, Dana was always impeccably dressed in the most up-to-date styles. That was why it looked funny, right now, to see her starting out the door in her shabbiest, most faded sweatsuit.

Faith put down her photography book and treated herself to a long, relaxed stretch. She was a pretty girl also, with her smooth dark skin and petite facial features. She usually wore her hair in a short, curly afro, which was very becoming to her. For a while this spring, with the arrival of a boy named Sheffield Adams, a sophisticated jazz trumpeter, Faith had switched to a smooth, uncurled coiffure. That style had been attractive, too, but Faith had gone back to her old hairstyle and her old self when she realized that she didn't want to keep up with Sheff's older ways.

"Wait for me!" Shelley, wearing jeans and a smart yellow cotton blouse, slipped into a trim navy blazer just before the girls left the room. She believed the blazer made her look slimmer, and Shelley was always looking for ways to look as slim as her two roommates.

Although, she thought now, as she eyed herself in the full length mirror on the door, she was certainly no longer the chubby, small-town Iowa girl she'd been last year, when she first arrived as a sophomore at Canby Hall. Her face was still mildly round and she had a few pounds that could have been pared from her hips — but she was an equally good-looking member of the trio, and much better at dressing chic, these days. She had learned a lot, being here at boarding school in Massachusetts. And that, basically, was one of the reasons why her parents had wanted her to have the experience of going away to school. Otherwise Shelley might have ended up married to dear, sweet Paul back there in Pine Bluff, without ever having seen what other options the world had to offer.

The 407 girls started up the flight of stairs toward Alison Cavanaugh's apartment, and were joined along the way by Casey Flint, their good pal from a room down the hall, an impish-looking towhead. Casey might have been the classic "poor little rich girl," if she allowed herself to be. Instead she was always ready for fun or mischief, she never bragged about her parents' wealth, and she was generally the one person you could count on to find out the gossip on any given subject at Canby Hall.

Tonight, however, she didn't have a clue about what was going on in Alison's penthouse apartment.

"Hi," Casey greeted. "So what's this meeting all about, anyway? I heard it's not just a social visit."

"Don't know yet, girl," Faith told her. "If *you* haven't found out — and you're our CIA Connection — then I guess we're just going to be in suspense until we get there."

At the top of the stairs they all stopped short.

There was a big, new, hand-lettered sign on the door to Alison's apartment:

"BEAUTY IS TRUTH,
AND TRUTH, BEAUTY ...
or, ABANDON ALL HOPE,
YE WHO ENTER HERE."

The four of them stared at the sign and burst into nervous giggles.

"Now what's that supposed to mean?" demanded Casey. "Dana — you're the poet. Do you read any obscure message in that craziness?"

"No," Dana said thoughtfully. "It's a combined, mixed up quotation from Keats, I believe, and from Dante's *Inferno....*"

The door opened, and Alison Cavanaugh stood there smiling almost mischievously. Alison, who was only in her late twenties, was unlike any other housemother at Canby Hall — and maybe anywhere.

She had long, sometimes wild hair of a reddish-brown color, and was known for her off-beat clothes, such as tonight's voluminous skirt from India, and the blouse with bold Navajo symbols all across the bodice.

Alison was different, all right, and very much loved by her charges in Baker House. Her apartment was always open to the girls (and now the boys) of her dorm, and she generally solved most problems in a single session, while fortifying all concerned with tea.

"Welcome." Alison motioned for the girls to enter.

"Are you sure it's *safe*?" Faith asked cautiously. "That notice on the door doesn't exactly make a person feel reassured, you know."

"Oh, it's perfectly safe," Alison said. "If you're a decent, honest person, that is." She emphasized the word *honest*, and winked in a most mysterious way.

The girls trooped in, looking around to see almost everyone else from Baker House dorm assembled on the couches and floor pillows of Alison's pleasant apartment. Even the three boys were there — the most recent additions to life at the girls' private school.

Sheff Adams, Terry O'Shaughnessy, and Keith Milton had been brought in that term as an experiment by the school trustees, to see whether turning Canby Hall coed would bring greater financial solvency to the school.

"Well, everyone's here now, I believe," Alison pronounced, after counting heads. "Folks, I'll be serving refreshments a little later — if your stomachs can be patient — but first, I want you all to meet my cousin, Maura Nevins. You can call her Maura. She's an undergraduate student at Boston University."

All eyes turned to the guest of honor, who smiled and waved a hand to the crowd. Interestingly, Maura was the exact opposite of Alison; she was small and dark-haired, and looked most studious.

"Hi, everyone," Maura said in a pleasant voice. "I imagine you're all wondering why I'm here, and why *you're* here, so I'll get right to the point. I came to ask your help — at least those of you who agree to my plan."

"Let me guess! You need us to help you play a prank on some sinister college professor!" That was Terry O'Shaughnessy, the acknowledged prankmaster of the school. "You came to the right place, Maura!"

Alison's cousin smiled. "I hope I did come to the right place, but no, this has nothing to do with pranks. It happens that I'm writing an important paper for my advanced psychology class, and I'm going to need teenage volunteers for a certain experiment."

"Oh, *no!*" gasped the irrepressible Terry. "She's planning to dissect our brains! Maybe even pickle them in sour dill juice. . . . Everybody knows what these psychologists do for fun. Aaargh, it's too awful to contemplate —"

"You can keep quiet now, Terrence," Alison told him firmly. "We all know you're a humorist, and believe me, if there were any brains to be pickled, you'd be the first one on the list. But I think we owe Maura the courtesy of listening to her, don't you?"

"This is getting dull already," came a bored voice from the plushest chair in Alison's living room. Pamela Young, the least-liked resident of Baker House, was yawning conspicuously and swinging her stockinged leg in a wide arc — very close to hitting Keith Milton's head.

Casey Flint was instantly alerted. She and Keith had, most surprisingly, fallen in love this semester, despite their many differences.

"Pamela dear." Casey Flint spoke up in a saccharine tone. "Just a word to the wise. If your foot lands on Keith's person in any way, you're going to find out rather quickly what it's like to be an amputee."

Maura turned to Alison, laughing. "My, you certainly have a talkative group here, Allie. I have a feeling they're going to be just perfect for the Truth Pledge."

* * *

Everyone in the room, with the exception of Pamela Young, sat up straighter with interest and anticipation.

"Truth Pledge?" Sheff Adams was the first to speak. "Man, what are you talking about? Sounds pretty official to me."

But Maura refused to speak until silence once again fell.

"Okay, in a nutshell, here it is: I'm looking for volunteers to sign up for a Truth Pledge . . . which means that for forty-eight hours you will tell the whole truth and nothing but the truth —"

"So help me, George Washington!" added Terry impishly.

"Well, why not? George Washington *is* a symbol of impeccable truth-telling," Maura agreed cheerfully. "And now, in my experiment, I want to try to determine whether it's possible for people of your age to be totally honest for that length of time . . . two whole days."

Dana raised her hand respectfully. "That doesn't sound hard at all. When would this project begin, Maura?"

"On Friday of this week. From Friday morning until Sunday morning. When the forty-eight hours is over, I will return to Canby Hall and ask each of you, in private, a series of questions about your experiences. It ought to prove to be very enlightening."

Alison stood up then. "Now, you must understand, nobody is required to sign up for this. But if you do — and I will appreciate it greatly, of course, that you're helping my cousin — then it will be expected that you *keep* your pledge. No matter what the consequences."

"So that's what the sign on the door meant," Keith Milton said in his quiet, scholarly voice. "You believe, Alison, that we'll be literally abandoning all hope if we pledge ourselves to this potentially explosive situation. Quite interesting." The brilliant Keith usually spoke like a pure scientist, as if his head were filled with computer software.

Alison smiled. She was as fond of Keith as everyone in Baker House was. "Well, yes," she admitted. "I think, knowing you kids as well as I do, that you could be treading into very deep and unknown waters, if you sign up. Now, what do you all think?"

Dana, Shelley, and Faith exchanged glances. They were such devoted buddies that each of them knew what the other two were thinking.

"No problem," Shelley said, speaking for the three of them. "We happen to be *very* honest people to begin with. We'll sign."

"Hah!" sneered Pamela from her throne-like chair. "If you three call yourselves honest, then *I'm* Princess Diana."

"I believe I'll sign," said Keith. "After all, truth and honesty should be an integral part of our existences." His phrases made Casey Flint smile. Keith was affectionately known as the dorm nerd because he was prone to intellectual philosophizing, and yet somewhat out to lunch when it came to social situations. He was famous for his mismatched outfits — plaids and stripes together, shirts that were too big or too small, and thick glasses that always needed a good dusting off.

"The project sounds like fun," Terry said, nodding his head thoughtfully. "I'll sign up. I guess I can go honest for two days without upsetting our national security."

Others all around were agreeing to join the experiment. The only dissenters, as far as Dana could see, seemed to be Pamela Young and — surprisingly — Casey Flint.

"Well, I think it's a waste of time," Pamela said, dismissing the whole project with a disdainful sniff worthy of her actress-mother. She was the daughter of the famous film star Yvonne Young, and made sure no one ever forgot it. "I personally never sign my name to anything of this sort."

"No, just to your credit-card slips in all the department stores," mumbled Terry, and all the kids around him rocked with laughter.

Dana stared at Casey, who was frowning. "What's the matter, Case? You having a problem with this truth experiment? You don't have to sign up if you don't want to."

Casey blushed. "Now that makes me sound like some kind of psychopathic liar, doesn't it? I guess I can manage to join, if the rest of you

can. It's just that —" She hesitated a minute.
"It's just that I'm always in some kind of hot
water as it is — and I wonder if this Truth
Pledge will end up boiling me alive, somehow!"

"Don't be silly," Faith whispered. "You
don't get into trouble anymore — not like you
used to." Faith, who was always the unofficial
"social worker" of the bunch — undoubtedly
a trait inherited from her mother, who was a
professional social worker in Washington,
D.C. — had helped Casey through a rebellious
period when she seemed to be in trouble more
often than not.

"Sign up with us, Casey. It's all for the sake
of science."

"That brings up a question," Dana said to
Maura. "I've always wondered — is psychology a true science?"

"Well, in my opinion, it tries to be," Maura
said honestly. "Psychology is still a relatively
new and uncertain science, of course. That's
why all of these research projects help — each
in its own little way — toward the understand-
ing of human behavior."

"Sounds mighty worthwhile to me," Keith
Milton said with enthusiasm. And that was
good enough for the Baker House crowd.
Keith might not have the social graces down
pat, but his opinion was respected by all.

Well, almost all. Even as the long sheet of
paper was being passed around for signatures,
and the majority of the crowd was eagerly

signing, Pamela Young stood up impatiently.

She yawned elaborately, and said, "I'm so sorry, Alison, but I can't be a part of this — this scene. I really have much better things to do."

"Yeah, like having reconstructive surgery done on her face," Casey snorted.

Pamela whirled around and directed a long, cold look at Casey.

"You'll be sorry you said that, Casey."

"Oooh, I'm really shaking in my boots," Casey countered. "This time, Pamela, you won't be able to get anything on me. I'll be involved in total honesty, you see?" Casey made a big show of putting pen to paper and signing her name to the Truth Pledge.

"Nevertheless, you'll live to regret your words." Pamela tossed back her long, blonde hair, put her nose into the air, and swept loftily from the apartment.

"Gosh, does anyone smell a skunk?" asked Terry, his freckled face full of innocence, as soon as Pamela had departed.

But there was an odd shadow across Casey Flint's face. She knew that Pamela didn't make empty threats. And she was wishing, suddenly, that she'd never agreed to sign the Truth Pledge.

As the students were signing their names, Maura called for their attention once again.

"I must say one thing more. You all act as if this were a joke." She spoke rather solemnly. "I do hope you know that the pledge requires total commitment, in order for my research to be accurate."

"Oh, *absolutely*," Shelley told her, and the others echoed her words. "We won't let you down, Maura."

Alison smiled in her mysterious way again. "You may think this is going to be easy, folks. But let me give you a word of warning: Complete honesty is a very difficult thing to achieve. And really, you may find yourselves in situations that — well, that may make you wish you hadn't pledged."

"Not *us*, Alison," Terry bellowed out. "How can you even insinuate that we Canby Hall people — such sterling characters — would even dream of being less than one hundred percent honest?"

"Well, we'll find out on Sunday morning, won't we?" Maura said. "I do want to thank you all in advance, because this project means a great deal to my grades — and my graduation. I want to wish you all good luck!"

"Good grief," Alison said, more to herself than to anyone else. "I wonder what this dorm is going to be like, for those forty-eight hours." Alison was still muttering as she went off to her kitchen for refreshments. "I mean, the place is a loony-bin all the time, as it is. What kind of little nightmares are going to result from a Truth Pledge?"

CHAPTER TWO

Friday morning dawned at Canby Hall, a crisp and sunny spring day laced with typical New England morning chill.

"Truthfulness," recited Dana, out of the blue. "Reality, veracity, fact, authenticity. Actuality. Gospel, accuracy. . . ."

"She's slipped her gears," Faith grumbled, poking her head out from under her thick down quilt. "It's finally happened, Shelley. Dana has turned into a walking dictionary."

"This is serious," agreed Shelley, but she was actually still under a heap of fluffy covers. She was reluctant to face the day just yet.

"I'm not reading the dictionary," Dana argued. "This is my thesaurus. Writers and poets use the thesaurus all the time."

"Oh, of course." Faith sounded as though she had to humor the deranged patient. "That explains everything."

Dana threw a stuffed teddy bear at Faith, who grinned and ducked. "I'm trying," Dana went on seriously, "to get us into the mood for the Truth Pledge . . . which happens to start in precisely one and a half minutes."

"This is Friday already?" From beneath her blankets, Shelley groaned. "Woe is me. I have that French test I've been dreading."

"You'll do just fine, Shel." Faith sat up and peered out the window that was near her bed — or to be more precise, her mattress on the floor. "Look at this — spring has really sprung here at Canby Hall. I've got to get going. I have a lot of seasonal pictures to take this week." One reason Faith had come to Canby Hall was to further her photography interests. She was so dedicated to her work that now she was the star photographer for the Canby Hall *Clarion*.

"Didn't you guys hear what I said before? The Truth Pledge experiment begins today." Dana looked at her bedside clock. "In fact, just about — now."

"No problem," Shelley said, finally peering out from under the blankets. "Haven't we already decided that we never lie? I mean, we are really very truthful people. We were all brought up that way. Look at Faith, for instance. Faith's father was a law officer and her mother's a social worker — it's obvious that honesty was an important part of her childhood."

"And you, Shelley," said Faith. "Growing

up in the Midwestern plains of America. . . . All Iowa people are straightforward, aren't they?" Faith wasn't teasing Shelley now; she seriously believed that Midwesterners were more sincere and down to earth than Easterners.

"Well, what about me? Aren't I just as honest as you two?" Dana looked somewhat miffed. "Just because I'm from New York, does that make me a low-down lying Manhattanite?"

"Of course not, Dana." Shelley tried to sound soothing. "That's what I've been trying to say. All three of us are truthful souls. So this Truth Pledge won't make the slightest bit of difference in our lives."

"No matter what Alison thinks," Faith added.

Shelley managed to heave herself out of bed, bleary-eyed. "I'll tell you something that's the honest truth — I'd like to sleep a few more hours. I did all that French cramming last night, even after lights out. *Pauvre moi.*"

"Up and at 'em, girl," Faith urged, even though she hadn't yet left her own bed.

"Casey sure seemed worried about signing the Truth Pledge, didn't she?" Dana observed. "I sure hope she won't get into any sort of trouble, because of it."

"I'm sure she won't," Faith reassured Dana. "I'm sure that none of us will. And I'm especially positive that our friendship can withstand any kind of truth-telling — about anything."

"Faith's right." Shelley's face broke into a grin, as it often did when mention was made of the girls' very stable friendship. Their bond meant a great deal to Shelley, who had thought, when she first arrived at Canby Hall, that she was going to die of homesickness, and would never adjust to boarding school life.

"The three of us can say anything to each other, and it wouldn't make a particle of difference. Let's try it."

Dana and Faith gave her a skeptical look, both frowning.

"No way," Faith said firmly, without hesitation.

"Shelley, let's not tempt fate, hmm?" Dana was frantically searching her bureau drawer for the other half of a pair of electric blue knee socks. At times like this she wished she was the neat, organized type, like Shelley.

Shelley was still persisting. "No, we wouldn't be tempting fate. I mean it. We ought to be brutally honest, just once, as part of the experiment. Go on — tell me something that you don't like about me!"

"I don't believe this girl," Faith said, shaking her head good-naturedly. "She must be a glutton for punishment."

"Aha!" Shelley pounced on Faith's words. "There — that proves it. There must be something you don't like about me — and you've been keeping it quiet all this time. Out with it."

"Shelley, no," Dana said firmly. "This is not what the Truth Pledge is really all about. It's not to rake up bad feelings. . . ."

"But if I ask, you have to answer me. And truthfully." Shelley's chin pointed upward in a defiant gesture. "Come on. Just one little fault. You first, Faith. You have to do it."

"I don't have to do it," said Faith. "I can refuse if I want to."

"I refuse, too," echoed Dana. "And now, let's start thinking about getting to classes, hmm?"

Shelley sat there defiantly. "I refuse to budge unless you tell me just one little thing that I've been doing wrong. I think it's healthy to clear the air, now and then."

Dana and Faith gave each other a meaningful look. Finally Faith said, "All right, if you're so insistent. There is one little thing, Shelley, old pal. At times I've wondered why it is that you always forget to buy shampoo — and then every morning you use ours?"

Dana nodded. "Yep. That's the only thing I can think of, too. And now can we forget this and get on with —"

Shelley managed to look very mature and thoughtful. "My goodness, I'm glad this came up. I never realized. I guess I just *am* forgetful, when it comes to shampoo, and I don't know why."

"It's okay, Shelley, really it is," Faith told her. "Don't worry about it. You're welcome to our herbal suds any old time. . . ."

But Shelley was worrying about it. "I believe I have something to say in my defense, though, girls. As I think about this — it seems to me that you two are always eating my goodies from home. So that ought to make us even, right?"

"That's absolutely right, it does make us even," Faith said. "Why, there we are pigging out on your mother's oatmeal cookies almost every week —"

"And you complain about a little bit of shampoo!" Shelley suddenly looked indignant. "Really, Faith, you ought to think before you speak."

"Shel, I didn't WANT to speak, if you'll recall!" Faith stood with her hands on her hips, looking as though she could be quite a dangerous adversary, even in her soft, lacy, pale blue pajamas.

"Enough of this." Dana spoke firmly. "We'll have no more True Confessions in 407. You see? It *can* cause hard feelings. Forget the shampoo. Forget the oatmeal cookies. We all borrow from each other, and it does even out in the long run."

Dana located her missing sock with a gleeful whoop. "Besides," she finished, "you never hear me complaining when you two help yourselves to my Halston perfume, do you?"

"I think we just did," the other two chimed.

Pamela Young swept into the dining hall and helped herself to a cup of strong coffee. She then strode deliberately over to the table where the girls from 407 and Casey Flint were sitting.

"Well, well," she said, seating herself gracefully. "I couldn't resist being with the four of you this morning, of all days. So the infamous Truth Pledge is upon you at this point?"

"Yes, it is, Pamela," said Shelley, trying to be decently polite.

"My, my." Pamela's beautiful face was contorted with amusement. "This is going to be ve-ry interesting. I really must remember to stay around to see all the fun."

"There's not going to be any fun, Pamela," Faith told her bluntly. "Contrary to what you may think, we are all very honest people around here. There's only one liar and troublemaker — and that's you."

"We'll just see about that when Miss Casey Flint starts getting into her usual trouble, won't we?" Pamela smiled sweetly. "And as for the rest of you — you're all such goody-goodies that you always say what people *want* to hear. White lies, in other words. And now, for two whole days, you're not going to be able to ooze all that politeness."

"Pamela, you're so low, you could do the limbo under a pregnant ant," Faith said casually as she cut into what was supposed to be French toast. Actually it resembled a rubber doorstop.

Pamela just smiled graciously. "I notice that Casey is mighty quiet this morning. I guess she doesn't know how to converse, when she can't tell falsehoods."

Casey was looking decidedly pale. She had stopped eating. The girls from 407 could see that she was scared witless of Pamela, for some unknown reason.

Pamela was still talking. "I intend to have the time of my life in the next two days," she said with great smugness. "It's nice to know that something interesting is finally about to happen here in Dullsville."

Faith decided it was time to rid themselves of Pamela.

"You know, girls, I think telling the brutal truth is going to be fun — when Pamela is around," she said, with a malicious look in her eyes. "There are a lot of things I've been eager to say about Pamela, for a long time now. Should I begin?"

"By all means," Dana prompted her.

Pamela's look of smug satisfaction disappeared.

"First of all, that hair color of hers," Faith said matter-of-factly. "Pamela claims it's her own color, but oddly enough, I've seen the exact shade — the exact shade! — in an advertisement for Miss Clairol bleaching products. . . ."

"What a coincidence," said Dana.

"That is totally untrue," Pamela snapped, but it was obvious that Faith had struck a nerve, somehow. "And besides, there's no excuse for rudeness." Pamela rose and left the table, abandoning her breakfast tea.

The girls all laughed when she was gone.

"Still, I can't help wondering what she's cooking up," Shelley said thoughtfully. "She can create a lot of trouble, and we all know it!"

CHAPTER THREE

Faith was right; spring really had sprung, Dana thought — quite unpoetically — as she walked briskly across the rolling lawns of Canby Hall toward her creative writing workshop. This day was going to be balmy and beautiful; already there was the sound of birds chirping in the maple trees overhead, and the sweet, moist smell of spring plants growing all around her.

Much as I love summer, she thought, *spring has got to be the best time of year. A time for new beginnings.*

And that reminded her of the short story she'd completed just in time for today's creative writing session. She had written a story about New York City, making it an optimistic, hopeful one. Maybe she was just in that frame of mind — upbeat.

Dana really enjoyed this class, and its competitive spirit. All the students in it seemed to be seriously interested in capturing good prose on paper, or good poetry images, as the case might be. And with her friend Terry O'Shaughnessy now in the class, it had become even more of a challenge. Terry was terrifically talented, in spite of being such a prankster, and his goal was to become a well-known writer someday.

Ms. Antonia Chase, who had been published in several top notch magazines, was their instructor. She was writing on the blackboard when Dana entered the classroom and took a seat next to Terry.

There had been a time, not long ago, when Dana had had a terrific crush on Terry, but it had turned out that he had a girl friend back home. Dana had had to re-evaluate her thinking about Terry, and about herself. It wasn't so bad to have a boy for a *friend*, she had decided; in fact, it was something brand new for Dana. The two of them helped each other with their stories and poetry, and really had a lot in common.

"Hi, there," Terry whispered, flashing Dana a big, impish smile. "How're we doing on this first morning of the Truth Pledge?"

"Just fine, thanks," she replied. "But we nearly had a casualty this morning with Shelley. She insisted that we tell her, truthfully, some one thing about her that bothered us. Can you get the picture?"

"Oh, no. Fatal mistake." But Terry looked amused.

"It sure was. All we did was tell her the simple fact that she forgets to buy shampoo, but she blew it up all out of proportion."

"Of course. It's hard for most anyone's ego to take the truth."

Dana thought about that. She supposed he was right, and yet — how could it be so? She and her roommates were not in the habit of telling lies. Not even little white lies, as Pamela had accused. Were they?

Ms. Chase called upon several students to read their work. Most of the stories were pretty good this morning, and the students evaluated them one by one, with criticism and praise.

Dana found herself daydreaming today, however, totally stabbed with a case of spring fever. She could barely keep her eyes away from the window and the bright, budding scene that was unfolding outside. It had been such a long, cold winter, she reflected. And it was such a pure joy now to experience the season's "fresh start," as their headmistress was fond of saying.

Terry O'Shaughnessy was called upon to read his story, and Dana forced herself to pay strict attention. She didn't want to miss one word of his work.

"*Holocaust . . . and a Half,*" read Terry,

pausing dramatically to indicate that this was the title of his story.

"Sounds like science fiction, Mr. O'Shaughnessy," commented the teacher.

"Yes, ma'am." Terry smiled, and began reading. He had a good, clear voice, and knew how to emphasize his words so that each sentence delivered the maximum impact.

But Terry, thought Dana, after a few minutes. *Your story is so depressing!*

She actually found herself fidgeting while he read his work. It was spring, for heaven's sake! How could he write about anything so bleak as the frozen aftermath of a nuclear holocaust on a far-off planet??

When Terry was finished, he sat down, and Ms. Chase invited comments from the class.

"Great writing," said Jackie Adams. "Really vivid imagery."

Another girl raised her hand. "Very smooth writing, I thought. It reminded me of one of Ray Bradbury's stories."

Dana had never read anything by Ray Bradbury. But she was surprised that no one else was saying what she was thinking — that the story had been a downer, especially at the conclusion.

"You're quiet, Dana," Terry said out loud, as though he were the moderator of the class and not Antonia Chase. "What'd you think of it?"

"Oh," she hedged. "I think . . . I'd rather not say."

Ms. Chase looked startled. "Why not, Dana? That's what we're all here for — to give constructive criticism. We'd like to know your opinion."

"Yeah," Terry said, sounding suddenly wary. "We'd like to know your opinion, Dana."

Stubbornly, Dana shook her head. "I'd rather not give my opinion on this particular work. I'm sorry, Ms. Chase."

The teacher frowned severely. "I'd be very sorry, too, Dana, if I had to give you a poor grade. You realize, of course, that one third of your grade is based on class participation. So it would be to your benefit, as well as Terry's, if you could provide us with an intelligent counterpoint."

Dana was defeated. She stood up and took a deep breath. "All right, if you insist upon my opinion, I have to give an honest one. This story . . . was so awful that it made me feel like throwing myself under a TRUCK!"

Terry looked amazed, and the rest of the class seemed to be shocked. But Ms. Chase just nodded and said, "Go on, please."

"Well," Dana said, feeling uncomfortable. "The writing, I agree, was excellent, as all of Terry's stories are. But the subject matter — and the way he hammered it home — gads, it was just so terribly negative, I wanted it to be over. I just wonder why Terry didn't write about the real world — and something a little more hopeful."

"A valid opinion," the teacher said, nodding her head. "Anyone care to comment on that?"

"I do." Terry stood, and there was an angry red flush making its way across his freckled cheeks. "I'd suggest that Dana learn a little something about this genre called science fiction, before she goes shooting off her ideas."

"Now, now, Terry, let's not get abusive —"

"Sorry, Ms. Chase. But this really burns me up, people running down a literary piece when they are too ignorant to know what they're discussing."

Dana caught her breath. Terry was really angry at her! She had never expected anything like this.

"You forced me to give an honest opinion," she said defensively. "I was only saying how I felt. . . ."

"Well, next time I'd suggest that you educate yourself, Dana, before you open mouth and insert foot." Terry sat down after delivering that cold speech. He refused to look at Dana for the rest of the class period.

Now I've done it, she thought. The Truth Pledge has gotten me into trouble already . . . and the day has hardly begun!

Faith, doing a frog dissection in biology class with Sheff and Casey as her partners, suddenly had a brilliant idea.

"Hey!" she burst out, almost knocking the

frog from the lab table. Casey made a violent lunge to keep it from falling.

"Watch it, Faith," Casey said impatiently, "or we'll lose all the work we've done on Kermit's digestive system."

"Oh, sorry." Faith put down her lab tools. She was too excited to think about biology at this moment. "You know what? I just realized, there may be a good feature story in this Truth Pledge thing."

"A feature for the *Clarion*? Hmm, not a bad thought." Sheffield Adams, tall and handsome and very, very smooth, was always in favor of anything to do with publicity. His goal in life was to be a jazz trumpet player, even though his parents, who were both doctors, wanted a more stable career for their son.

Sheff struck a theatrical pose. "How's this, Faith? Do I look like the very essence of honesty and forthrightness?" He flashed a devastating smile. "I'll pose for a truth picture any time you want."

"I'll just bet you will," Casey mumbled, pushing both of them out of the way. "I can see that if anyone's going to do any work here today, it's going to be ME. Excuse, please."

"Oh, Casey, I didn't mean to desert you," Faith said sincerely. "I'll pay attention to Kermit's small intestine — honest."

"Yeah, *honest*. That's what's got us all tied up in knots today," Casey complained. She did look nervous and uptight today, there was no denying it.

"Are you letting Pamela upset you, Case?" Faith asked. "Because if you are, that's crazy. She can't do anything to hurt you."

"She always manages to hurt someone," Casey said. "And this time she swore it was going to be me."

"I know but —" Faith stopped because their biology teacher, Ms. Henderson, was wandering down the lab aisle, watching for anyone who might be goofing off. The three heads — Casey's, Faith's, and Sheff's — suddenly were bent over their work with an eagerness that hadn't been there before.

"Anyway, I hope you get a good *Clarion* story out of all this," Casey whispered to Faith. "There ought to be a few humorous things going on. In spite of Pamela's evil doings...."

Faith was still thinking about her possible photo-essay on the Truth Pledge when she left the science building later. Sheff had to walk fast to catch up with her.

"Whooa, wait up there, little lady," he called, in his best imitation of a cool musician type. "What is your hurry?"

"Hi, Sheff." As always, when she was with Sheff, Faith felt less sure of herself. She had been flattered by his attention when he first arrived as a student at Canby Hall; and yet, at the same time, Sheff was the sort of guy that she had always tried to avoid — the smooth, well-dressed, overly confident type. It was a mystery to Faith just *why* she'd ever been attracted to Sheffield Adams . . . but even now, once in a while, it was still there.

"So. How are you doing with the Truth Pledge so far, Sheff?" she asked, looking up at his luminous dark eyes and feeling a slight knot of excitement in the region of her stomach.

"Piece of cake," Sheff bragged. "I don't tell too many lies anyway. I do like to tease my roommates, by telling them outrageous stories, but I'll just forgo that for two days."

Sheff's roommates, of course, were Keith Milton and Terry O'Shaughnessy. They were the only three boys in the school. They'd been housed in the basement rooms of Baker House in a suite that once belonged to the maid, way back in the early, more gracious days of Canby Hall.

Canby Hall had been founded in 1897 by a wealthy industrialist, Horace Canby, when his only daughter, Julia Canby, died of fever at a young age. In tribute to Julia, Mr. Canby established a girls' school on the property that would have been her inheritance.

Although the school had grown considerably since 1897, there was much that had remained the same as the original estate, especially outdoors — the wooded paths and picnic areas, the skating pond, and the summer house that was still located near the residence of the headmistress, Patrice Allardyce. And in the birch grove was an important part of every Canby Hall girl's experience — the statue of the lioness with her cubs, donated by the class of 1917 to symbolize the strength of womanhood.

"Did you say you don't tell *many* lies?" Faith repeated. "That means you do tell some? That's a shocking admission to make, Sheff."

"Oh baby, don't act so holier-than-thou." Sheff reached out and brushed a wisp of hair from Faith's forehead as they walked along. "Everybody tells some kind of lies from time to time. I hope you aren't deluding yourself that you don't."

"I don't think I'm deluded, and I certainly don't think I ever lie — in any form." Faith knew she was speaking in a prissy tone, but she couldn't seem to help it. She was convinced that she was telling the truth.

"Hey, suit yourself," Sheff said, shrugging. "But how about this for complete honesty? I'd like to take you out to dinner tonight. How does an evening in Boston sound?"

Faith stopped walking and, to her surprise, felt a slight stab of disappointment. "Sheff, that sounds tempting, but I already have a date. I'm sorry." And she was, too, even though she had long ago decided that Sheff was not the guy for her.

"A date with who? That insignificant little town boy — the one who plays baseball? What's his name? Jimmy? Joey?"

"It's Johnny Bates, and you know it." Faith frowned.

"Well, Johnny then. Give me a break. That guy is strictly Nowheresville, Faith. You and I have so much more in common."

"We do?"

"Of course. I'm into music and you're into photography — and those are two forms of art. We have glittering futures ahead of us, Faith.

"Come on, Faith, break that wishy-washy date with what's his name, and step out with me." Now Sheff put a possessive arm around Faith, and she found herself shivering, for some reason. "Let me be really corny and say — we could make such beautiful music together."

Faith couldn't help but smile. "No, I'm sorry, Sheff, but I can't break the date. I promised Johnny, and the whole gang, and I never let my friends down. But maybe some other night?"

"We'll see, Faith. We'll see." Sheff seemed to pull back, both physically and emotionally, and Faith could sense the chill in his new mood. "I might be busy myself, some other night."

And before she could reply to that, he was off in a different direction, heading toward the library with a long-legged stride. He was whistling softly, as though the matter had been totally forgotten already.

I'm getting just as bad as Shelley, Faith

thought, and gave a kick to a clump of new grass that was sprouting up along the campus path. *I know I like Johnny better, and yet I get swept away, now and then, by this Romeo with his talk of Boston and the arts. . . .*

Shelley had been torn between two boys ever since sophomore year, when she'd gotten a role in the spring play and had fallen for the handsome male lead, Tom Stevenson. Back at home, in Pine Bluff, Iowa, she had Paul waiting for her. Paul was a small-town person like herself and had planned to marry Shelley in a few years.

Faith and Dana had laughed many a time over Shelley's fickle indecisiveness about these two boys. And now Faith was horrified to find herself in the same predicament!

Sheff was so devastatingly handsome and full of charisma that Faith found it hard to resist him. And she really tried.

But Johnny Bates was lovable and hard-working and loyal, and just the type of really great person that Faith's father had been. A lump came into her throat every time she thought of her dad. He'd been killed in the line of duty as a police officer in Washington, D.C., several years ago.

But if she cared so much for Johnny Bates, then why did she have such a reaction whenever Sheff issued an invitation?

I won't think about that now, Faith decided, heading toward her next class. She'd get her mind working on the new feature story for the *Clarion*. She knew that if she just kept her eyes open — and her camera handy — she'd see problems springing up all over Canby Hall . . . among the people who had pledged to tell the truth.

And I'll get the best story ever done for that newspaper, she vowed.

She'd prove to herself that there was a lot more to life than juggling two boyfriends, who both happened to be fascinating, and both jealous of each other.

CHAPTER FOUR

"Everybody ready for another gruesome gourmet meal?" asked Casey Flint, stopping by Room 407 at a few minutes before noon. Casey loved 407, and not only because of the three roommates. It was a unique room because the girls had painted the walls black early in the school year. They'd also dispensed with their bedframes so that their mattresses sat on the floor, creating a cozy, casual atmosphere.

"Lunchtime already?" Dana said. "My, time does fly. . . ."

"When you're having fun," finished Shelley. "And it certainly was fun, taking that French test this morning. Especially when I was feeling rather upset about a certain shampoo incident. . . ."

"I hope you're kidding," Faith said, "because you know darn well that you *forced*

36

that so-called shampoo incident. So if we have to hear about it for the rest of this semester, *Shelley.* . . ."

"Okay, okay!" Shelley backed away. "I *was* kidding . . . sort of. Anyway, the matter will now be forgotten. History. Ancient history. And I'll never ask for a truthful report again — from anyone."

"Good." Dana was shedding her heavy sweater and replacing it with a more spring-like cotton blouse. "Because that truth-telling really can get you into trouble. I should know."

"What happened to you, Dana?" Casey asked, leaning against the door jamb. "Did Pamela cause you some grief?"

"Pamela? No. It was my own doing." Dana made a face that showed she was truly disgusted with herself. "When Terry read his story in Creative Writing Workshop, I was told I had to give my opinion, so I did. And then Terry got really angry at me!"

"I take it you weren't crazy about his story," Faith commented in a dry tone.

"No, it was hideous. Made me shiver, you know? But apparently Terry isn't the kind who can accept constructive criticism."

"Well, let's get a move on. I'm hungry," Casey said, "even if we do have to eat at Ye Old Torture Chamber dining hall."

The four friends chatted on their way to the dining hall, which was next to Canby Hall's main building. Actually, the dining hall was an attractive enough place, with a whole wall of windows and sunlight, and a veritable garden of hanging green plants.

No, the girls had no complaints about the way the dining hall *looked*. It was just the food that was the butt of all their jokes . . . and it was agreed that most of the food, except for the salad bar, was pretty bad.

"Uh-oh," Casey mumbled as they neared the entrance to the building. "That's Pamela waiting there by the door. She's up to something — I just know she is!"

"Casey, you're getting absolutely paranoid," Dana said. "You don't have to be afraid of —" But before she could finish, Casey had turned on her heels and disappeared behind a big forsythia bush.

Faith looked surprised. "Gosh, Casey sure is skittish about Pamela these days, isn't she?" she commented to Dana and Shelley.

"I don't know why." Shelley shook her head as though Casey were being quite juvenile. "What in the world can Pamela do to hurt anyone, even if we are bound to truth-telling?"

"Hello there, girls," called out Pamela in her sweetest voice. Dana could tell, right off, that Pamela had been waiting there just for their arrival. "I have a monumental surprise for you all."

"A surprise," Faith repeated in just the same sweet tone. "Isn't that lovely of Pamela, to arrange a surprise for us?"

"I guess Casey was smart to take off when she did," Shelley mumbled.

Without another word, the three of them tried to brush right by Pamela, but Pamela blocked their way.

"How unfriendly of you, *mes amies!* Really, and when I've gone to so much trouble to help you in your Truth Pledge."

"Move it, Pamela, or lose it!" Faith said brusquely. "We're going in for our lunch."

"Of course you are. And that's what this surprise is all about." Pamela stepped into the dining hall right along with them. "I believe you all are acquainted with this lady over here?" With a dramatic gesture, she pointed to a small, white-haired woman in an apron who was standing by the start of the self-serve line.

"Hi, girls," the woman said, beaming brightly. They recognized her, of course, as Mrs. Merriweather, the head cook.

"Er, hi there, Mrs. Merriweather," Shelley said uneasily.

"That's right," Pamela went on. "She's Mrs. Merriweather, our cook, and do you know what? I've told her about your Food Grievance Committee."

"Food Grievance Committee! What are you talking about, Pamela?" Dana looked truly angry now, and she didn't often lose her temper.

Mrs. Merriweather walked happily over to the girls. She wore spotless white shoes, like a nurse, and her kitchen uniform was starched and sparkling.

"Pamela explained to me how you three want to help out with suggestions about the food." The cook seemed to be very pleased with the idea. "I can't wait to hear what you have to say, girls. I want to know just what you think of my meals."

Three jaws dropped in horror.

"She . . . she wants to know what we think of her meals," whispered Shelley.

Dana cleared her throat. "Pamela is mistaken, Mrs. Merriweather. We've never formed any committee."

"No. Not us." Faith was nodding her head in agreement.

But Mrs. Merriweather was not one to be stopped by small details. "Committee or not, I am still thrilled by the whole idea," the cook said. "I really want your help with this. I even told Ms. Allardyce how pleased I am, and she agreed that you should cooperate."

"She did?" Shelley asked in a sinking sort of voice.

"Yes. Why, I think Pamela Young was just wonderful to think of this. . . . Well, where *is* Pamela? She must have gone in to lunch. . . ."

Sure enough, Pamela had disappeared. Her evil plot had been successfully hatched.

What, thought Dana, were they going to DO? They couldn't possibly tell Mrs. Merriweather, honestly, what they thought of the dining hall food! They just couldn't!

But they couldn't lie, either.

Is this where a white lie would come in handy? Dana wondered, but only briefly, because they had to do something . . . immediately.

"Would you like to be a real committee," asked Mrs. Merriweather, "and step into my office? I have a nice office right down the hall, where I make out my menus."

"Oh no, no — thank you." Faith was the only one of the three who was thinking fast enough to take action. "Listen, Mrs. Merriweather . . . this is a bit premature. We need a little more time to think about our, um, suggestions."

"That's it! I mean, that's right," said Shelley gratefully. "We need more time. A committee can't just rush into things. . . ."

"Exactly." Dana nodded very solemnly. "We'll just have to get back to you at some later date, Mrs. Merriweather."

The elderly woman looked disappointed. "Well, all right, but definitely tomorrow, at lunchtime. Pamela said you'd want to speak to me before Saturday night."

"Oh sure. She would say that," muttered Faith.

Glumly, the three roommates headed for the salad bar.

"I'd rather be shot at dawn than try to eat that gloppy entree in there that she calls stew," Dana said. "Boy, Casey sure was smart to run away from Pamela — and lunch."

"We'll think of a way to handle this," Faith said, but she didn't sound too convincing. "Maybe we can avoid Mrs. Merriweather until the Truth Pledge is over."

"Not much chance of that," Shelley argued. "She'll come in search of us — probably with bloodhounds, if necessary. Didn't you hear how eager she was to talk to a grievance committee? Oh, this is a nightmare!" Shelley raised the back of her hand to her forehead in a highly dramatic gesture. Her two friends stared at her, realized that she was being serious, and they burst out laughing.

"At least your theatrics help us to keep our sense of humor, Shelley," Dana said with great affection. The tension had been broken. The three friends shrugged and began heaping their bowls with plenty of nutritious raw vegetables, beans, and cheeses.

"Dana?" A timid voice spoke up from behind Dana. "I see that Casey isn't here."

Dana turned. It was Keith Milton, Casey's short, nearsighted, and thoroughly lovable boyfriend.

"Hi, Keith. No, I don't think Casey will be coming to lunch today. This Truth Pledge really has her spooked, for some reason."

Keith's solemn face didn't change. "That's all right, Dana, because it was you I wanted to talk to. Do you mind? I have something to ask you."

Surprised, Dana just nodded. She told the others she'd join them later, and she walked over to an empty table to sit with Keith.

"What's up, Keith? You and Casey aren't having trouble, are you?" The two had become an item ever since Keith had tutored Casey with her math, and it was a romance that the whole school seemed to applaud — in spite of the fact that Keith was a head shorter than Casey.

Keith grinned. His whole face seemed to light up when he smiled, and even the thick, dusty glasses and tousled hair failed to make him look like a nerd at such moments. "There's no trouble, Dana. Casey and I are doing just fine. That's why I wanted to ask you a favor." He hesitated only for a second, and then blurted out, "Can you teach me how to be more fashionably coordinated?"

Now Dana was really startled. But she caught Keith's meaning after a moment. He wanted to learn how to dress well, to look sharp — instead of like a refugee from a physics seminar.

"Of course I'll help, if I can," Dana said gently. "Is there any special reason why you want to dress . . . um, differently all of a sudden?"

"Yes." Keith almost blushed. "Casey's birthday is next week, as you probably know, and I was thinking that I'd like to take her out, to some really nice restaurant in Greenleaf, for a birthday dinner. And Dana, I don't want her to be ashamed of the way I dress. . . ."

"I understand." Dana put out a reassuring hand and patted Keith's fidgeting fingers. "Clothes make the man, they say. I don't know if that's true, and I think you're a terrific man, but if you want to be 'fashionably coordinated,' then — that's what we'll aim for."

"Thanks, Dana. Would you be able to visit our downstairs suite sometime today, and look over what I have?"

"Well, can I be truthful?"

"Of course. In fact, you have an obligation to be, don't you? This is one of the Truth Pledge days."

"Right. Well, I've seen most of your clothes, Keith, and frankly — I think we might do better to start out from scratch. Begin at square one — at a clothing store. Do you have enough money to get a whole new outfit?"

"I sure do." He smiled again. "My grandparents sent me a hefty check just for clothes, when I came to Canby Hall. And I haven't spent any of it yet."

"Great. Then why don't we go into Greenleaf soon — tomorrow, if possible — and look around the men's shops there?"

Keith pushed his chair back. "Sounds wonderful to me, Dana. And listen, don't tell Casey anything about this, will you? I want everything to be a total surprise."

"You've got it."

"Thanks, Dana. I can't tell you how I appreciate this."

What a really nice boy he is, Dana was thinking, as she said good-bye to Keith and carried her salad plate back over to the table with Faith and Shelley.

How lucky Casey was, she went on thinking, to have found a gem like Keith!

CHAPTER FIVE

Shelley, leaving her last class of the day, was struck with a glorious attack of spring fever. The air smelled sweet and sharp, the trees looked so tender with sunlight filtering down through tiny new leaves that she was reminded suddenly of home. And that made her happy, not homesick, because she really did love Canby Hall and the friendships she'd made here.

Impulsively, she decided to take a short, brisk walk through the woods before going back to Baker House. She was glad of her decision when she heard birds chirping merrily and was even treated to the sight of a mother rabbit with three fuzzy, adorable little babies.

As she emerged from the woods along a path that was lined with ferns, she realized that she was heading toward the formal gardens that lay behind the house of the imposing headmistress, Patrice Allardyce. It was an area that students never invaded.

Oh, well, what the heck? Shelley thought. Nobody'd ever been *forbidden* to walk here, she supposed. Old Horace Canby wanted all of the school grounds to be available to the girls of Canby Hall. They'd heard that line often enough during the Wednesday morning assemblies that P.A. — the girls' nickname for Patrice Allardyce — always gave.

Shelley was fascinated by the size of the long, fenced-in garden. She'd heard that Ms. Allardyce had a lovely flower garden here, and even did some of the gardening herself, but of course Shelley had never had the opportunity before to see firsthand.

Nothing ventured, nothing gained, she reminded herself, as she slipped through the garden gate to take a quick peek at the tulips, which were in full bloom. The garden was beautiful! Tulips of every imaginable shade contrasted against the darkness of the rich Massachusetts soil.

Shelley pulled her head up abruptly when she heard something.

A strange sound, almost like a groan, made it obvious that Shelley wasn't alone in the garden. Had she imagined the sound? There was no one in view. Reluctantly, she walked on farther, toward the other end of the garden.

"Help me . . . someone. . . ." This time she knew she'd heard it! Shelley raced toward the voice, and found a figure lying flat on a path of flagstones.

It was Ms. Allardyce.

"Shelley Hyde, is that you?" The headmistress was able to talk, but she sounded as though she was in pain. "I need your help."

Shelley bent down, and was shocked to see the bleached whiteness of the headmistress' face. Ms. Allardyce's blonde hair, which was always pinned perfectly in place, was now a tangle of loose ends and full of bits of peat moss from where she was lying.

"What can I do, Ms. Allardyce?" Shelley asked in what she hoped was a comforting, reassuring voice. "Shall I call an ambulance? Or should I run and get the nurse?"

"No, no." The woman spoke with extreme difficulty. "I don't want anyone — This is not a matter to be made public."

"But . . . what's wrong, Ms. Allardyce? Did you fall? Do you have any broken bones?"

The headmistress tried to sit up. With Shelley's help, she was able to do so, but she still looked pale and drawn.

"I'm having some chest pains, that's all," she said.

"That's all?? But that's quite serious. . . ."

"Perhaps. Perhaps not. At any rate, I would like to go to Greenleaf Memorial Hospital, Shelley, but I don't want the whole school knowing about this."

Shelley felt her own heart begin to thump in her chest. Here she was, confronted with a major problem, and she wasn't sure how she should handle it. Shouldn't she disobey Ms. Allardyce's command, and go for help anyway? Alison would know what to do, or Miss Zenger, the school nurse.

"Shelley, can you drive a car?"

Oh, no. Shelley guessed what was coming next. And she was tempted to say no so that she could run for outside help. But it was one of the Truth Pledge days, and Shelley knew that she couldn't tell a lie — even for a noble cause.

Reluctantly, Shelley said, "Well, yes, I can drive, but — I have a license from Iowa. I don't ever drive here in Massachusetts."

Patrice Allardyce was sitting straight up and getting ready to stand. She was evidently well enough to worry about her appearance, because she brushed at her navy blue gardening slacks and, at the same time, whisked away some of the debris from her hair. "Well, good. Then you are going to drive my car, and take me to Greenleaf Hospital."

Shelley almost choked! Patrice Allardyce had always been a very remote figure to her. She was a frosty, mysterious person whom Shelley and almost all the students feared and avoided. Ms. Allardyce was a woman to respect, yes, but a woman you never expected to encounter, face to face, unless you were in dire trouble at Canby Hall.

And now Ms. Allardyce was expecting her

— Shelley Hyde — to drive her into Green-leaf, to the hospital!

"I . . . I don't know, Ms. Allardyce. I probably should get one of the teachers to drive you . . . *please?*"

The headmistress regained a semblance of her cold, firm manner. "I told you once, and I won't say it again: I don't want anyone at Canby Hall to know that I am ill."

With that, she managed to get herself up, leaning heavily on Shelley and on part of the nearby picket fencing. "There. I can get to the car, I'm sure of it. And you'll find my keys, Shelley, in my purse. In the house on a table in the front hall."

I don't believe this is happening, Shelley thought wildly. She was really frightened. The whole thing was impossible. Suppose she was unable to drive Ms. Allardyce's unfamiliar car? Or worse, suppose the headmistress became really sick while they were on the road? What would Shelley do then? She didn't know anything about first aid for a heart attack victim!

"Let's go, Shelley." Ms. Allardyce was commanding her; she really had no choice in the matter. And maybe the best thing was to move quickly. Maybe the woman's very life depended on Shelley obeying without question!

She helped the ailing headmistress to walk, slowly but steadily, to the huge garage that housed the Buick Regal. Shelley raised the wide garage door, and helped Ms. Allardyce settle herself into the passenger seat. Then Ms. Allardyce instructed Shelley again to run to the house for the purse and keys.

Shelley found herself saying a little prayer as she followed instructions. *Please, please, don't let anything serious happen to her ... especially not while I'm in charge here!*

She entered the elegant home by the front door, spotted Ms. Allardyce's snakeskin purse right away on an antique marble-topped table, and grabbed for it. There was no time to lose.

And then she was sitting in the driver's seat, beside Ms. Allardyce, fumbling with the key ring and wondering how in the world this fancy car ran. It certainly was different from her father's old station wagon ... or Paul's pickup truck.

But something inside her took hold, saying that she had to summon strength — and competence. She could handle this, she really could. Because she must.

"Here we go then, Ms. Allardyce," she said, hoping she sounded confident. With the very first try, the powerful Buick engine came to life, its motor roaring with a smooth rhythm.

Shelley did just fine, backing the car out of the garage, and then the driveway. She began to feel capable.

"You seem to be a good driver, Shelley," Ms. Allardyce told her, but the woman's face was pinched with pain and she wasn't really watching how Shelley handled the car.

"I think I'll close my eyes," the older woman said wearily. "I can relax, now that you're in charge. I know everything will be fine."

That built up Shelley's confidence even more. It was important, she realized, to make Ms. Allardyce feel at ease, so that her heart could be at rest. So — Shelley was an aspiring actress, wasn't she? She could put on a convincing act of being a very experienced driver. And that's exactly what she did — the whole way into Greenleaf.

It seemed like the longest ride in all eternity. Shelley never noticed any of the scenery that flew by — the hills and fields, the farms with their silos and barns, the little country churches and schools that dotted the countryside. She just kept whispering her little prayer, over and over, as she sneaked little sideways glances at Ms. Allardyce.

Finally, she reached Greenleaf. She pulled neatly up to the sign that said HOSPITAL EMERGENCY ROOM, and leaped out to go for a nurse. Several hospital personnel emerged, one bearing a wheel chair, and from then on, the problem was out of Shelley's hands.

She went inside, of course, to see how she might be of help. While the medical people whisked Ms. Allardyce away, Shelley tried to answer a few of the questions asked by the Emergency Room clerk.

Then she sat down on a hard wooden bench to wait.

After what seemed an eternity to Shelley, Ms. Allardyce had finally summoned her to the little curtained cubicle in the Emergency Room.

"This is an inconvenience to me, Shelley, but nothing more," Ms. Allardyce had said, lying there on the examining table, looking pale and sick. But she was just as full of self-control as ever. "But it is very important that you get this straight. For reasons of my own, I do not want the students or the staff at Canby Hall to know about my illness. Do you understand, Shelley?"

"Of course, Ms. Allardyce." Did the headmistress think she was absolutely dumb, that she had to keep repeating her orders to Shelley? "I won't tell anyone, if that's the way you want it."

"Thank you. My secretary, Peggy, won't be looking for me, as tomorrow is Saturday, and my housekeeper is out of town for a few days, visiting a relative. So there should be no one who will really put up a big fuss about my absence."

"But . . . suppose the houseparents have to contact you for any problems?"

"They can handle anything that comes along, I'm sure." Ms. Allardyce began to look extremely tired, and Shelley realized that she shouldn't be bothering the patient with hypothetical questions.

"Of course. Everything at Canby Hall will run very smoothly, Ms. Allardyce. All you have to do is concentrate on getting well. And don't worry about your car, either. I'll park it back in your garage."

"Thank you, Shelley. I want you to hold on to the keys, so that when I'm released — whenever that may be — you can drive back here to pick me up. Would that be all right with you?"

"Oh yes, of course! I'd be very honored to come for you. I'm very honored, as it is, that I was able to help you."

"Young lady, you'll have to leave now," a nurse said crisply. "Your headmistress is quite exhausted, and we want to get her up to her hospital room just as soon as possible."

"I'm going. So long, Ms. Allardyce. And — please get well soon."

She thought she saw the ghost of a surprised smile on Ms. Allardyce's usually austere face, at that. *Why, she's just a human being, like all the rest of us*, Shelley thought. And she responded to regular old human kindness, Shelley thought further. It was a good thing Mrs. Hyde had instilled such good manners into her daughter, because they sure had come in handy today, in helping to make a sick lady feel less alone.

CHAPTER SIX

"Where in the world is Shelley?" Faith was the first one to ask that question. The Baker House girls were poking along through the self-serve line at the dining hall, staring dismally at the latest dinner concoction of Mrs. Merriweather and her crew.

"This must be Friday night. Fish night," Casey grumbled. "You are looking at a reincarnation of Orca the Whale there on that platter. Served in bubbling blubber-base broth."

"Gross." Dana made sure she whispered her comment, so that the cook wouldn't hear. She didn't want to be held accountable for any complaints if she really had to be on a grievance committee.

"Well, where *is* Shelley? Does anybody know?"

"It's not like her to miss a meal," Dana commented. "But then, since we're all going to the Tutti-Frutti later with the boys, maybe she decided to skip this Orca treat."

"I can't help worrying about that girl whenever she's late," Faith said, moving along down the line toward the small dishes of Jell-o.

"I'm sure she'll show up soon," Dana said as they sat down to supper. "How much trouble can she get into? This is Truth Pledge time, remember? Nobody can pull any dishonest tricks — except Pamela, who never signed."

"Oooh, don't remind me of that Pamela!" Faith stabbed at her tuna salad plate viciously, as though she could see Pamela Young's face there in the mayonnaise. "I could kill her for that deal with the cook. And we still don't know how we're going to get out of it . . . tactfully."

"How are you coming with your story for the *Clarion*, Faith?" Casey asked. "Got any good stuff about the Truth Pledge yet?"

"Not yet," Faith admitted. "Of course Dana got Terry mad at her, but I don't want to write about that. And Shelley was pretty huffy about the shampoo, but —"

"You don't want to write about that, either." Dana chuckled. "It sounds like all the things that happen are going to be too personal, Faith. Too private to publish in the school newspaper."

"Maybe." Faith smiled confidently. "We'll see. I'll just go on keeping my eyes and ears open — and maybe a big story will break."

Just then Mrs. Merriweather spotted the girls and waved, with a big wooden stirring spoon clenched in her hand. "Don't forget," she called out gaily. "Tomorrow for sure! I can't wait to hear from the committee!"

Keith Milton was whistling happily as he came padding out of the shower in the boys' down-stairs suite. He was wearing a robe that was two sizes too large and was the greenish color of a seasick lizard.

"Do you have to be so doggoned cheerful, Milton?" Terry grumbled, not looking up from his writing desk. Terry was working on a new story for Creative Writing Workshop, but looked as though he was hating every minute of it.

"Why, certainly," Keith said, smiling and conducting a nearsighted search for his eye-glasses. "Because I *am* cheerful this evening. I have a date with a very sweet lady . . . Casey."

"I'm glad somebody around here has a date," Sheff said grudgingly. "I made my bid, but Faith still plans to stick with Dudley Do-Right, the future policeman. Well, it's her loss."

Sheff was lounging across his bed with his trumpet, which was affectionately nicknamed "Babe," but he hadn't been practicing any music. He was just glaring off into space, thinking about Faith and her loyalty to Johnny Bates. It was infuriating to him. It baffled him, when he knew that Faith was really attracted to him, Sheff, and his more sophisticated ways.

"If you ask me, *all* Canby Hall girls are losers," Terry said grimly, and his two roommates turned to stare at him, shocked. Terry's face was actually flushed red with anger.

"What's eating you, man?" Sheff asked lazily.

"Aaah, it's that Dana." Terry slammed his notebook closed. "I thought she was a decent person. I thought she was a friend."

Keith shook his head solemnly. Without his glasses, he looked like a nearsighted tree owl. "Dana Morrison *is* a very decent person. And she certainly is a trustworthy friend. To what specific problem are you alluding, Terry?"

Terry picked up another manuscript. "I am alluding to this — my sci-fi story that I read today in writing class. The whole class liked it, and understood what I was trying to say. It's a warning type story; you know, telling humanity to be careful or we'll end up living in the aftermath of a holocaust. But does Dana understand? No."

"Some people don't dig that kind of fiction, Terry," Sheff told him. "And you can count me as one of them. I don't want to hear any of that Gloom City futuristic stuff."

"'That's not the point," Terry said. "Any serious student of creative writing should be open to all kinds of genres. You're a musician. I wouldn't expect you to understand."

"Did Dana offer her opinion in class?" Keith asked. His hand had just clamped down on the glasses that were perched on top of his overflowing desk.

"Well, she was sort of forced to give it. Ms. Chase made her. But then Dana really went overboard and said a lot of negative things — and I'm still furious with her."

Keith put on his glasses and observed Terry thoughtfully. "Would you rather she had told a lie? After all, this is Truth Pledge time."

Terry looked even more annoyed. "No, I wouldn't rather have had her tell a lie! But she could have said, 'I don't understand science fiction,' instead of all that rude business she did say."

"What do you care what she thinks, anyway?" Sheff asked.

"I don't know why, but I do care. Or I did. Dana's a good writer herself, and I valued her opinion. I thought she had some intelligence about literature — and also about people's feelings."

Keith frowned. Usually Keith said very little to his roommates, especially in the way of advice. But this time — maybe because of the Truth Pledge — he felt he had to speak up.

"If you don't mind my telling you the truth

as I see it," he began, "I think you're being quite childish about this matter."

Terry blew his stack. "I do mind you telling me the truth!" he snapped. "But as long as you started it, I might as well tell *you* the truth. You may know a lot about the sciences, Milton, but not a thing about life. Or girls."

"I wouldn't quite say that." Sheff had an amused lilt in his deep voice. "Don't forget, there are two of us stuck hanging around the dorm tonight. Milton's the only one with a date tonight, as far as I can see."

CHAPTER SEVEN

By seven o'clock, Shelley still had not appeared.

"Not even a note from her," Faith said, as she poked around Room 407 for some sort of clue. "She knows we worry about her; why would she do this?"

"I wonder if we should go to Alison?" Dana mused. "She might know something. On the other hand, we might be getting Shelley right into some sort of trouble, if we rat on her. . . ."

"She couldn't have left the campus," Casey told them, "because she didn't sign out. I checked Alison's sign-out list, and her name's not there. And Shelley's not the type to sneak off. Now if it were me who was missing. . . ."

The friends laughed. "Then we'd really have to wonder. Good old Casey could be anywhere!"

"Well, the boys are probably downstairs by

now," Dana said. "I'm sure Shelley will turn up for her Tutti-Frutti date with Tom Terrific."

In the Baker House lounge, a huge room full of warm-toned oak paneling, sat the four boys who were planning on a trip to the ice cream shop. Tall and lanky Randy Crowell was Dana's special friend. Although he was the most handsome boy she'd ever seen, he was a real country boy whose life revolved around farming and raising horses. Randy came from a large family of landowners there in Greenleaf, and he was content to be a horseman and forgo college.

But because Dana was such an incurable city girl, their friendship was just that — a nice, warm friendship. They made no pretense at being in love, these days, and they were comfortable together.

Keith Milton was waiting for Casey, and was dressed in his usual scattered way — a striped shirt, much too large, and a strange pair of "highwater" jeans. But Casey never cared about Keith's clothes, any more than she worried about her own. She was just glad she'd found someone who really liked her, and that the feeling was mutual.

"Hi," called out Tom Stevenson, who was Shelley's date. Those two had been going together for almost a year now, and they still cared for each other quite a bit. "Where's Shelley?" Tom asked now.

"We're not sure," Dana said. "We thought maybe you'd know."

"I don't." Tom shrugged. "All I know is, we have a date tonight."

"Sounds like you're in need of a good detective here." That was Johnny Bates, the fourth boy of the group, and he was waiting for Faith. Like Tom, he was a town boy, and attended Greenleaf High School. Next year he planned to study at the law enforcement academy, with hopes of making his career as a police officer. Johnny was dark and handsome, with a great sense of humor, and he was crazy about Faith Thompson.

"I guess we'll just wait here in the lounge until we hear from Shelley, hmm?" Dana looked at Tom, and then at Randy, for confirmation of this plan.

"Fine with us. We're in no great hurry," Randy said. "We can probably find a great Western movie on the TV."

"Oh, you and your horses!" Dana knew he was teasing her. But she sat down beside him on the sofa to wait for Shelley.

"If nobody minds, Keith and I are going to start walking into town," Casey said, holding Keith's hand.

"We are?" asked Keith.

"Sure. We have some stuff to talk about."

Oh ho, thought Dana. *She wants to grill him about our little talk today at lunchtime. Well, she's out of luck! Keith won't tell her, either, why we were having that conference.*

"Go ahead," Faith said. "Hopefully we'll meet you at the Tutti-Frutti in half an hour or so, as soon as Shelley shows up."

Dana whispered, "You're probably leaving just in time, again, Case. I do believe I hear Pamela Young coming down the stairs right now."

"Then we're outta here!" Casey yanked Keith by the arm and sped out the door. She wasn't taking any chances on Pamela during these forty-eight hours.

"What's going on around this place?" Randy looked puzzled. "Why is everybody afraid of Pamela all of a sudden?"

"Well. . . ." Dana was just about to tell him about the Truth Pledge, when the infamous blonde bombshell from Hollywood made her grand entrance. She was dressed, as always, in dramatic attire — a bright gold lounging robe that swept across the floor as she walked, and a matching gold band holding back her hair.

"*I'll* tell you exactly what's going on." Pamela's eyes had that gleam that everyone recognized as T-R-O-U-B-L-E.

"Oh good, you're all here," she gushed, looking around at the crowd of boys and girls. "All except Shelley, I see. Well, no matter. What I have to say is to you townies. . . ."

"You want to talk to us, Pamela?" Tom looked wary. He was always eager to know what was going on at Canby Hall, especially if it concerned Shelley in any way, but he knew, as well as the others did, that Pamela Young was not to be trusted.

"Yes indeed." Pamela settled herself loftily on the arm of a stuffed chair. "I wonder if any of you are aware, yet, of the Truth Pledge that is under way in Baker House."

"Never heard of it," Randy answered, sitting back in his usual relaxed way. "Suppose you tell us, Pamela. You're going to, anyway, I gather."

Pamela's face was flushed with glorious excitement. "Why, it's just simply this, boys: Your girl friends have pledged themselves to complete honesty . . . for two whole days. And this is one of those days. So — can you just imagine the possibilities here?"

"Frankly, no, we don't know what you're getting at, Pamela." That was Tom, who looked again at his watch and was obviously wondering what could be keeping Shelley.

"Just think of it, boys! You can ask the girls anything — anything at all! — and they must give you an honest answer. No tact, no evasions, and no cutesy little lies."

Randy was the first to laugh heartily at Pamela. "Gosh, it just boggles the mind, doesn't it, men?"

"You can laugh. But if you miss out on this opportunity, you'll never again have the chance. *Real, honest answers to your questions!*"

Pamela stood up and brushed at a tendril of hair that was falling across her pretty forehead. "Especially you, Johnny, because, whether you know it or not, Sheff Adams is still always trying to coax Faith to go out with him."

"No, I didn't know that," said Johnny quietly. He turned his soft brown eyes toward Faith.

Pamela knew she'd scored on that one. "Don't be fools, boys of Greenleaf. This is your big moment."

Then she swept out of the room, leaving a trail of expensive perfume in the air behind her.

"What a total birdbrain she is!" Randy exclaimed. "Does she really think we consider our girl friends to be liars? I never heard of anything so dumb."

They all laughed, except Johnny Bates. He was standing stock-still, and staring at Faith with an odd expression on his face. Finally he said, "Um . . . Faith? Can we go outside and talk, just for a few minutes?"

Faith slipped into her light spring jacket and went out into the balmy night with Johnny. They started walking along the path toward the campus gates, just because they usually enjoyed the scenery on the way to the lioness statue.

"You want to ask me something, Johnny?" Faith sounded a little shaky, though she didn't know why. She was hoping that maybe he just wanted a quick hug or kiss. Although kissing on the campus was strictly a no-no, it was a rule that was often broken after the setting of the sun.

"I guess so." Johnny looked a little sheepish as he walked along under one of the pole lights. "Faith, did you sign that Truth Pledge the way Pamela said?"

"Why, sure. We all did — except Pamela. It's for an experiment in psychology, and it's —"

But Johnny interrupted her, something he rarely did. "Does that mean that if I ask you a question, you'll answer me truthfully?"

"If I can," Faith said, her voice coming out in rather a whisper. "But I'm always honest with you anyway, Johnny. Don't you know that about me?"

"Well, I do believe that you are — to a point. But Faith, there's something that's been bothering me for a while now . . . ever since that trumpet-playing bozo arrived as a student here at Canby Hall. . . ."

"You mean Sheff Adams," Faith said flatly.

"Right." Johnny stopped walking, and he shuffled his feet rather nervously. "You know how you went nutsy about him at first, and you changed your whole image? Eye makeup and that smooth new hairdo, and — all kinds of things that made you look different."

"I suppose I did do some of that, Johnny, but I got over that a while ago! Look — here's my same old afro, back again. And the same old me in my sweatshirt and jeans."

Johnny reached out and touched Faith's hair gently, just for a moment. Then he pulled back, and Faith saw an odd thing in his eyes — a sadness that she had never seen before.

"Faith, I really need to know where I stand. As I said, it's been bothering me for a while now. So I think I'd like to use this opportunity, if you don't mind, to ask for the truth."

"What truth, Johnny?" Faith felt that her heart was somewhere up in her throat, because she was having such trouble breathing. She didn't like the way this was shaping up, not at all. She shouldn't be forced to make any choices. . . .

"I just want to know, plain and simple. Do you have any interest in that Sheff Adams, or not?"

"Oh, Johnny. . . ." She put out her hand, because she was so touched by the pain in his voice, but he pulled away even farther.

"No, really, Faith. No evasions now. I think I'm entitled to an honest answer."

"Of course you are." But that was all Faith said for a while.

"Well?" He was standing there with his hands jammed into his pockets, looking very forlorn.

"You've taken me by surprise. I have to think of just the right way to say this, Johnny. . . ."

"If you have to think so much about it, then

I guess we have a real problem, don't we, Faith?"

"No! That's not it at all. It's just that you're asking me for total honesty, and I'm trying . . . oh, I don't know how to say this. It's a matter of being dazzled, I suppose, by the glamor and sophistication of Sheff Adams. . . ."

"That much I know," Johnny grumbled.

"Yes. Well, it's also because — when I'm with Sheff, he represents a very different world, the world of the jazz musician. And that's a part of the whole sophisticated arts scene that lies ahead for me, as a photographer."

"Big deal. You're talking about ten years or so down the road, Faith. What does that really have to do with now?"

"Oh, I don't know how to answer that, Johnny. With you — well, I feel happy and comfortable, because we've been dating each other for so long. But I know that you're going to be a policeman, and that still does bother me. Though I try not to let it. . . ."

Faith had tried, for a long time, to come to terms with Johnny's plans to become a police officer. Her father, Police Officer Walter Thompson, had been killed in the line of duty, trying to stop a bank robbery, when Faith was ten. Those terrible memories and fears didn't go away too easily.

"So you do like Sheff better, then," Johnny concluded. "I guess I always knew it, but I wanted you to say it outright."

"Oh, no, Johnny. . . ." But Faith's protest was too late. Johnny had already turned away from her, and was walking along the quiet, darkened path alone.

Suddenly, he stopped. "I'll talk to you soon, Faith," he called out, "but for tonight — I'm not in the mood for ice cream, anymore. I think I'm going to walk on home."

Faith watched him as he left, his head held high to hide the emotions he was feeling. She just didn't know how to smooth things over. What could she say to him, other than making up a tactful little lie?

Desolate, she turned herself toward Baker House and made herself start to walk briskly. She passed the statue of the Canby Hall lioness and her cubs, bathed in the pale, fading light, and she gave a disgusted, lionlike snarl.

"Fat lot of good you do anyone," she mumbled to the lioness. "You're supposed to be the symbol of the strength of all womanhood. And what am I? A wimp who wants to hide behind some white lies just so she won't have to face any decisions."

"What's your hurry, Faith?"

Faith was startled to see Sheff Adams striding along beside her, his long legs moving faster than she could ever hope to.

"Where in the world did you come from?" she demanded.

"I've been out here strolling and feeling lonesome."

"Were you . . . were you listening to Johnny and me?"

"I might have been. I might have heard the end of a certain conversation." Sheff's face was lit up with a big, happy grin.

"You shouldn't have eavesdropped. I can't think of a worse thing to do!"

"Oh Faith, girl, don't start that lecturing now. This is a big breakthrough, thanks to the Truth Pledge. Now I know that it's me you really care for." He put a long arm possessively around her shoulders. "So that makes it official. You're my chick from now on."

Faith stared at him. Sheff suddenly looked so smooth and so smug that she was shocked. Why, compared to Johnny, who was utterly sincere and always had been, Sheff was a real phony.

Why hadn't she seen that before?

"Come on, baby. Forget about that little nobody. Now you and I can enjoy Boston together, concerts and jazz shows, and you with your 35-millimeter camera always ready. . . ."

How tempting it all sounded, when Sheff put it that way! She had always wanted to see more of Boston, and the many cultural attractions going on in that city.

But Faith pulled away. She was haunted by the sad look in Johnny's eyes.

"Truthfully, Sheff, I don't want to be your — 'chick.' Or your 'baby.' *Especially* not your baby." She spoke slowly, but she was sure of what she was saying. "I really like Johnny a great deal. I just couldn't seem to explain things to him."

"Don't give me that, Faith," Sheff started to say, but Faith was no longer listening. She was walking back to Baker House, alone.

"Oh, I hate this truth-telling!" Faith howled, storming back into the lounge where Dana, Randy, and Tom still sat waiting for Shelley.

Dana knew that something serious had happened. She was just about to whisk Faith off toward the dorm kitchen, for a private talk, when Ginny Weissberg, one of the girls from Baker House, came running into the lounge.

"Will you all come out here? This minute —" Ginny burst out, looking upset and worried. "Hurry up — especially you Dana, and Faith. . . ."

Immediately, without a question, everyone leaped up and followed Ginny. The summons was too urgent to ignore. Even Pamela, who had been standing around in the Ping-Pong room, apparently, went rushing outdoors to see what was so momentous.

"Over this way. Hurry!" Ginny called out, running with unusual speed, for her, toward the driveway of the headmistress' house.

They all stopped when Ginny pointed dramatically to the car that was pulling slowly into the driveway. Although it was a semidark night, the burgundy Buick Regal was clearly visible as it purred quietly along under the campus lights.

"So?" Faith was the first to lose patience with Ginny. "What's the big deal? That's P.A.'s car. We've seen it a hundred times before."

"But wait until you see who's driving it. All alone," Ginny said, still wearing that worried frown.

The whole crowd of them watched as the car stopped at P.A.'s garage, and a lone figure got out to open the garage door.

It was Shelley.

CHAPTER EIGHT

"But Shelley, you *have* to tell us why you were driving P.A.'s car." Dana looked absolutely distraught. "Oh, I can't believe I'm even saying that! You, driving Ms. Allardyce's car . . . alone, and at night. . . ."

"Shelley, please. What kind of trouble are you in? Maybe we can help you!" Faith hovered over her friend, and was actually wringing her hands, like a character in a TV soap. Forgotten were all thoughts of Johnny Bates or Sheff, and her own problems with truth-telling. This was much more serious.

The girls were closeted up in Room 407 now, having dismissed their dates a while ago. Nobody was in the mood for ice cream at the Tutti-Frutti anyway.

"Tom was upset, too, you know," Dana went on. "He probably thought you were out joyriding with the headmistress' car. But you weren't, were you, Shel?"

Shelley laughed without humor. "No, it sure wasn't a joy ride."

"So what was it?" Faith asked.

"I can't tell you that," Shelley said slowly.

"What do you mean you can't tell us?" Dana demanded.

"Yeah," Faith said. "We're your best friends. You can tell us anything."

"No, I just can't," Shelley said.

"I don't believe you," Faith said. "You're not only lying to your best friends, but on Truth Pledge Day, too."

"Okay. You two look like you've reached the end of your patience," Shelley observed. "I can tell because you're about to slip a hangman's noose around my neck; that usually indicates a serious breakdown in communication."

"Ha ha. Very funny." Dana folded her arms across her chest, waiting.

Shelley looked at both of them, straight in the eyes. "I am telling you the truth. The truth is, I can't *tell* you the truth. And I refuse to tell you a lie, on this of all days. So there you have it — I can't tell you anything."

"Shelley —"

"Look. Read my lips. I-CAN-NOT-TELL-YOU-A-THING. If I could, I would, you know that! I've never kept secrets from you before, have I?"

"Has she?" Dana asked Faith. It seemed to Dana that there had been several instances when Shelley had kept things from her roommates, and usually it involved Shelley being in some kind of scrape — such as the time she was secretly dating Randy, for instance, behind Dana's back. That hadn't lasted for long, but at the time it had been a major problem between the two girls — and upsetting for the confused Randy, as well.

And there had been the time Shelley was sneaking around, just before the spring trip to Fort Lauderdale, going to a reducing salon called Heavenly Bodies so that she could trim her thighs for wearing a bikini.

But neither Dana nor Faith reminded her of those incidents. They were too worried about this horrifying, puzzling mess.

"You know that Pamela saw you, as well as half of Baker House," Faith pointed out shrewdly. "You don't think that old Pamela is going to let this rest, do you? She'll be the first one to rush to P.A. and tell her!"

Shelley shrugged. "Let her, then. I can't help it."

"But Shel," Dana wailed. "You could be expelled from Canby Hall for something like this. It's the worst rule infraction I can ever remember anyone ever doing — even including some of the things Casey has pulled!"

"Look, I really can't talk about this anymore. You'll just have to trust me, on the basis of our friendship. Well, that's all I have to say to you two right now."

Faith made a choking sound. Dana's eyes almost popped out of her head.

"You're serious, Shelley? You want us to trust you and not ask any more questions?"

"That's exactly what I want. Because I can't answer you anyway." For the first time, Shelley looked a bit frazzled and pale, as though something had upset her quite a bit today.

"Are you okay, Shel?" Faith could see, suddenly, that they had been pushing their friend a little bit too much.

"I will be," Shelley answered wearily. "Look, isn't there something we could do — to get our minds off all of this? How about a game, or a snack, or going down to watch a TV movie?"

"I'll bet you had no dinner, Shel." Dana became aware, too, that Shelley had been under some kind of severe stress. "Would you want us to forage around the dorm and see who has any decent food? Maybe some peanut butter and crackers, or some fruit?"

Shelley sank down on her mattress on the floor, looking pale and tired. "Wow, that sounds good. I guess I am hungry, Dana. Somehow I knew. . . ." She looked up at them with tears in her eyes. "I knew that you two wouldn't condemn me, even without knowing the facts. I guess you really are the best friends in the whole world."

Dana thought that tears were going to spring into her eyes, too. "We'll dig up a feast for you, Shelley. And we'll tell the rest of the girls to mind their own business. They're all hanging around outside, hoping to get some answers, you know. But we'll straighten them out."

"Right!" Faith agreed. "It's no one's business except Shelley's. And she'll tell us about it some day — when she can."

"Thank you, guys," Shelley said simply.

Telling the girls of Baker House to mind their own business was easier said than done. As soon as Dana opened the door to Room 407, about thirty faces were staring at her, eager for news.

"What did Shelley tell you?" asked Ginny Weissberg. "Is she in real trouble, or what?"

"How can we help, Dana?" That was Cheryl Stern, always thoughtful of other people in the dorm.

"Why did she do it?" demanded Nancy Plummer. "What's going to happen to her, if P.A. finds out?"

Dana sighed deeply and closed the door firmly behind her. "Hey, gang, this is really a mob scene here, you know? I realize you all mean well, but Shelley has a problem that none of you can solve. And you're not going to get any answers from me, or anyone, about why she was driving that car."

"We're not?" Ginny sounded terribly disappointed. "Why?"

"Because Shelley has a right to privacy. And she doesn't have to be considered guilty until proven innocent."

"That's ridiculous, Dana," pointed out Heather. "We all saw her committing the crime. . . ."

"Look, you guys, I don't want to get angry, but I've had enough. Please — just forget it. I mean, just forget the whole situation for now. And what you can do to help —" Dana turned to Cheryl and Ginny. "You can all scrounge up some food for Shelley. All donations will be welcome."

The crowd looked crestfallen, but they had enough respect for Dana to stop the questions.

"What food have we got on hand?" Cheryl asked.

"I've got some bananas in my room," Dorothy Hicks offered.

"I have peanut butter and jelly," Heather said.

"Come by my room," Maureen Cassidy said. "I've been hoarding some candy bars for a special occasion. I guess this is it."

Dana suddenly felt like giving every single girl a big hug of gratitude. They must be the best bunch of dormmates in the whole world!

Laden with goodies from the whole dorm, Dana was starting up the first-floor stairs when

Keith and Casey arrived back from Greenleaf.

"Hey! You guys never showed up at the Tutti-Frutti," Casey called out.

"Nope. But we found Shelley, anyway," Dana said. The tray she carried was piled high with bananas, yogurts, brownies, and even a plateful of Alison's newest health-food creations, prune granola cookies. "I'll tell you all about it later, Case."

"All about what?" Casey looked intrigued. She was torn between wanting to spend the rest of the evening with Keith, and wanting desperately to rush up to Room 407 to hear the latest news flash.

Dana stopped on the stairs, looking resigned. "Might as well tell you, briefly. Shelley came driving back to campus — nobody knows where from — all alone in Ms. Allardyce's car."

For a moment there, it looked as though Keith and Casey were going to fall over with real shock.

"*P.A.*'s car," Casey repeated, with a weird sort of calm. "Shelley? Our Shelley? Michelle Hyde from Pine Bluff, Iowa??"

Dana nodded. "And don't ask me any more than that, because that's all I know . . . honestly."

"Truthfully and honestly!" Casey howled. "Everyone's been so honest today it's making me sick. Why can't we all just go back to the way we were? Why did we ever sign that stupid pledge, anyway?"

Dana stared. "Why Casey, the pledge hasn't hurt *you* in the least. I'm the one who's got Terry mad at <u>me</u>, and now Faith is afraid she's lost Johnny forever, and. . . ."

Casey made a quick decision. "There's a lot going on in 407, Keith. I hate to say this, because I'd love to be with you all evening, but . . . good-bye."

"Aw, I understand," Keith said mildly. "I'll go downstairs and hit the books. Or beat Sheff in a chess game."

Casey flew up the stairs, two at a time, after Dana, helping her to carry the food supply. She never even got started asking questions when her nose picked up the scent of Pamela Young's overpowering perfume, again, this time coming toward them on the stairs.

"Here comes the Dragon Lady," murmured Casey almost under her breath.

"Feeding your faces again, I see," was Pamela's comment as she brushed past them on the stairs, bumping deliberately into Dana and almost making her spill the food tray.

"Not that it's any of your business," Dana said, "but this is for Shelley." She said it defiantly, to show her loyalty to her roommate.

Pamela laughed. "She's going to need a lot more than that. She's going to need a cake with a file baked into it, in the place where she'll be going . . . prison. After she's expelled from this dismal school, that is."

It had never occurred to Dana that Shelley had committed a legal offense as well as a

Canby Hall misdemeanor. What if Ms. Allardyce pressed charges? Would Shelley end up in reform school?

If only we could keep anyone from knowing about it, Dana thought, *so the police wouldn't have to be notified....*

"Pamela," she began in her nicest voice. "You don't really want to see Shelley get into that kind of trouble, do you? Isn't it possible that you could just forget what you saw tonight?"

"You have got to be kidding," Pamela said, her big blue eyes looking innocent. "Even though I didn't sign the Truth Pledge, I wouldn't dream of withholding the truth. P.A. must be told about this matter, Dana. I'm simply shocked at you for suggesting otherwise."

Dana sighed as she watched Pamela marching on down the stairs, no doubt on her way right then to Ms. Allardyce's house.

"The Wicked Witch of the West strikes again," Casey said through clenched teeth.

"She's right in one way," Dana said slowly.

"What do you mean?"

"We'd all be willing to lie for Shelley. We'd all do anything we could to keep Shel out of trouble. I'm beginning to see that we're not quite as honest as we thought we were."

"Who cares?" Casey groaned. "Let's just get this food up to poor, starving Shelley. And if I don't hear all these latest stories immediately I'm going to turn into a pumpkin!"

CHAPTER NINE

I t's a nightmare," Casey declared a half hour later, after the 407 girls had filled her in on everything. "I knew the Truth Pledge was going to bring us all bad luck! I just knew it!"

"That will be over in another day," Faith said quietly. "The bitter truth is, we've each got problems that we caused ourselves, it seems to me. And Shelley's is the biggest of them all."

"No kidding," Casey said grimly. "Shelley could be in really big trouble if Pamela starts shooting off her mouth. Why am I saying *IF*? She's probably at P.A.'s house right this minute, telling all. . . . Doesn't that worry you, Shelley?"

"Don't put pressure on her, Case," Dana said gently. "She looks like she's been through enough."

"Enough *what*?" Casey wanted to know. "What would make a perfectly ordinary girl like Shelley steal a car? And take it for a ride somewhere? And the car of the headmistress of Canby Hall, no less?"

"Maybe Shelley had amnesia," Faith suggested, but not too hopefully. "Is that it, Shel? Or did you have a case of temporary insanity? A lawyer might be able to get you off on that plea."

"I cannot tell a lie," Shelley said, unable to resist giggling. "I'm as sane as any of you are."

There was a knock on the door.

"I told those girls in this dorm we weren't going to answer any questions," Dana said grimly, going to answer the knock. "Whoever that is, she's just being nosy."

She opened the door to see Terry O'Shaughnessy.

"Terry!" she greeted him happily. "It's so good to see you! You must have heard that we needed a friend tonight. . . ."

"No, Dana," Terry said coldly. Dana felt suddenly as though a pail of ice water had been thrown over her. So he was still peeved about this morning in writing class!

"I'm only here to relay a message." Terry spoke precisely and frostily. "I just came from The Penthouse, where Pamela Young was on her way out, and Alison said she needed me to bring a message to 407."

"Let us guess." Faith spoke in a dry tone. "Alison wants to see Shelley — at once."

"That's right, Faith." Terry's face softened when he looked at the other girls in the room — and his eyes avoided Dana. "Gee, I hope it's not something terrible."

"It is," Dana said. "But why would you care? You're too busy holding a grudge over something so silly and juvenile."

"My writing career is neither silly nor juvenile, Dana," Terry answered in an acid tone. "I happen to be very serious about it. Well, good luck, Shelley — whatever the problem is."

"Thanks, Terry," Shelley said, looking resigned.

CHAPTER TEN

W ell, young lady." Alison was waiting for Shelley at the top of the stairs, looking more than a little distressed. "Please come in, Shelley. I won't even put on the teapot until we've talked about this — this incredible thing that Pamela has told me. Because of course I don't believe a word of it. . . ."

Sighing, Shelley entered the apartment. Alison motioned for her to sit down on the long sofa with all the embroidered pillows. It was a beautiful room, warm and colorfully decorated. All the girls agreed that Alison had the best decorating taste they'd ever encountered. There were potted floor plants, and hanging green plants, art exhibit posters, and great magazines always on the coffee table. One whole wall had been lined with bookcases.

It was a place where Shelley had always

loved to come with her troubles, no matter how large or small. But tonight she was in a real dilemma because she couldn't tell the true story of Ms. Allardyce being in the hospital.

"Well?" Alison sat down, too. "I'm waiting, Shelley."

Shelley held up both hands helplessly. "I'm afraid it's true," she said simply.

"What?" Alison looked as though someone had just thrown her into a pit full of snakes.

"I suppose Pamela told you that I was driving a car. Ms. Allardyce's car. Well, that's true. I was."

"Heaven help us all," Alison breathed, her shoulders suddenly sagging. "Shelley, why? What possible reason could you have had?"

"Believe me, Alison, I do have a reason. A good one. But I can't tell you what it is, not without lying."

"Lying? You're worrying about the Truth Pledge at a time like this? Shelley, all I *want* is the truth — and then maybe I can help you."

"You can't help me, Alison. Except maybe by having faith in me. You know I wouldn't do anything wrong."

"But you have done something wrong, Shelley, don't you see that? This is the most incredible act of disobedience that I've ever come across, in all my time as a housemother."

Shelley bit her lip to keep herself from speaking. She alone knew that she hadn't been disobedient. But how could she possibly hope to make anyone understand? Ms. Allardyce had sworn her to complete secrecy.

Alison continued to cross-examine Shelley until she, too, like Dana and Faith, realized that it was no use. She was not going to get the story out of Shelley Hyde.

"Well, Shelley," Alison said, "it seems that Ms. Allardyce is not around this evening, or so Pamela tells me. Pamela went over to her house but everything was dark. I don't know where Patrice can be, but of course you know that I'll have to confer with her when she does return."

"Of course." Shelley hoped that that would be very soon. She was beginning to feel the effects of the unfairness of this situation. All she'd done was help the headmistress, and here she was, practically a convicted criminal, at least in many people's eyes.

"Until that time, I'm going to have to ground you," Alison said regretfully. "I have no choice, Shelley. And I have to make it a severe grounding. You can't leave Baker House at all, except for meals in the dining hall."

"Oh," Shelley said in dismay. "But I have a real special date with Tom tomorrow night!"

"No, I'm afraid you don't. At least not until Patrice decides what is to be done, and we get to the heart of this matter."

"Okay," Shelley said in a small voice.

"I don't want to do this, Shelley — not to

you." Alison looked almost as though *she* were going to start crying. "But you do understand, I have to take some action. Ms. Allardyce is going to be livid."

No, she's not, Shelley thought dismally. But aloud, she said, "Don't feel bad, Alison. I understand. Really I do."

"I won't take this picture if you object, Shelley." Faith was standing outside The Penthouse with her camera aimed at the door just as Shelley came out. "I know it's ghoulish of me, but I'm trying to get photos of these two days — the effects of the Truth Pledge. And somehow I think your problem falls into that category."

"Oh, all right. You can take the picture, Faith," Shelley said in her most tragic, dramatic voice. If she had to be a martyr, at least she might as well be a good actress about it. "But I might not want you to put it in the *Clarion*, you understand."

Quickly, Faith snapped several candid shots in a row, before Shelley could change her mind. These pictures would be dynamite, Faith was thinking: Shelley Hyde, in the biggest school trouble of her life, emerging from a session with the disciplinarian housemother.

Now this was the stuff that news stories were made of!

The only trouble was, Faith knew that she probably wouldn't submit her roommate's picture to the newspaper. You couldn't capitalize on one of your best friend's misery.

"Well, if nothing else, this photo-taking gives me something to do, to keep from thinking about Johnny." Faith sighed deeply as the two girls started down the stairs toward Room 407.

"Oh, Faith, here everyone's been worrying about me, and you've got a big problem of your own!" Shelley was genuinely sympathetic. "What's going to happen? Do you think you'll really lose Johnny, after all you've meant to each other for so long?"

"I don't know, Shel." Faith spoke quietly and it was obvious that she was deeply concerned about Johnny's feelings. "I'm not sure he can ever forgive me. And all I did was try to tell the truth."

"Bless the good old Truth Pledge," said Dana, overhearing the last part of their conversation as they came near the room. "It sure has made life fun for us all, hasn't it?"

"Yeah. Terry's really annoyed at you, isn't he?" Casey observed. "How are you going to remedy that?"

"I have no idea. The truth still stands; I don't like the story he wrote."

"And what's the bad news with you, Shel?" Casey asked.

"Grounded, of course. No date tomorrow night with Tom. And we were going to see a really special play at a community theater!"

"Bummer," Dana said, sounding depressed.

"Well, I'm going to make us some tea," Faith said firmly. "This is a sad-looking group if ever I saw one. We need a tea lift."

"We can drink a toast to the Truth Pledge," Casey grumbled.

"Yeah," Shelley agreed. "And we can hope that maybe tomorrow will be better!"

"It can't possibly be any worse, can it?" asked Casey. "Unless Pamela finds a way to carry out her threat to get me. . . ."

"There's nothing Pamela can do to you, Casey, if you keep your nose clean." But Faith didn't sound so certain now. After all the things that had been happening, she wasn't certain about anything anymore.

CHAPTER ELEVEN

"H ey, sleepyhead. How about a game of Frisbee?" Keith Milton was calling to Casey, who was sleeping fitfully in her fourth-floor room. She was dreaming of Buick Regals and Shelley as an armed, masked car thief with Pamela Young sitting on the hood pointing a gun at her.

"Huh?" Casey yelled, startled. Where was the voice coming from? She groped her way to the window and looked down at the grassy meadow that stretched out behind Baker House. Through the newly budding leaves of the ancient maple tree, she spotted Keith.

"Hi!" She waved her arms enthusiastically out the window. The thick branch of the beloved tree was so close to her window she could almost touch it. "What're you doing up so bright and early?"

"I need exercise," Keith said. "Been studying half the night. Now it's time to spin the old Frisbee."

"Studying half the night?" Casey mumbled to herself, realizing once again that Keith was not like most other boys. He was the kind of kid who could sit and read an advanced calculus textbook as though it were a fascinating novel. Not for the first time, she wondered what such a brainy human being could possibly see in her.

Casey had no illusions about being a great beauty or a Miss Congeniality. She knew she was stubborn, often tomboyish, and usually quite casual about clothes and makeup. She had, however, changed in many ways since coming to Canby Hall.

She didn't pull giant temper tantrums anymore. She didn't brood when her busy parents had "no time" for her; she was learning, with the help of her good friends, to be more sociable and cheerful. And she had improved herself, perhaps subtly, simply by watching — and imitating — the sophisticated, fashionable ways of Dana; the strong, no-nonsense qualities of Faith; and the country-style good nature of Shelley.

"Well, it looks like a gorgeous morning out there," Casey called out. "I guess I could use some exercise, too. See you in a few minutes." Secretly, she was overjoyed. She'd never had this kind of easy companionship with a boy, and it was a wonderful feeling. She felt, oddly enough, as though some sort of magical door had suddenly opened up for her, so that now Casey Flint was just like so many of the other sixteen-year-olds everywhere — a girl who could appeal to a boy!

She joined Keith out on the back lawn, and was surprised that he gave her a shy good-morning kiss — and not on the cheek! Usually he wasn't too demonstrative, especially not in public places.

"Let 'er rip!" she called out to Keith, getting herself ready for some serious Frisbee playing. Keith took the game as seriously as he did chess, and calculus, and everything else he tackled. Keith was no halfway kid, about anything.

They enjoyed a half hour of the game, feeling buoyed by the signs of spring that were everywhere, all around them. Casey could smell lilacs blooming from a spot near a stone wall, and she was delighted with a row of vivid yellow daffodils that were bobbing their saucy heads along the brick foundation of Baker House.

So all was happiness and light, until, without warning, trouble arrived. Bernard Kreevitch, the groundskeeper, came ambling along a path that led from the gardener's shed. Mr. Kreevitch was carrying a giant chain saw.

"What the heck?" Casey blurted out, dropping the Frisbee and following Bernard with her eyes. He was heading right toward the maple tree that grew by her dorm window!

Mr. Kreevitch stood for a minute, looking up at the tall tree, and then gave a shrug, as if to indicate that this was no difficult job for an experienced outdoorsman like him. He began to wind a long, thick rope around the circumference of the maple.

"What do you think you're doing?" Casey growled, marching over to him.

Mr. Kreevitch looked at her in surprise. "Why, I'm doin' what Ms. Allardyce told me to do, of course. The tree has to come down. The power company is complaining that the branches are growing right up against the power lines — see up there?" He pointed and Casey's eyes followed his finger. Sure enough, anyone could see that the tree was dangerously close to the electric wires.

"But you *can't* cut down this whole tree!" Casey was adamant. More than that, she was horrified to think that anyone would even consider taking away one of her favorite things at Canby Hall — the maple tree that was like one of her very own closest friends!

"Sorry, Miss," Mr. Kreevitch said politely. "But what Ms. Allardyce orders, I have to do."

"I won't let you!" Casey sprang into action, throwing her body up against the maple tree with a fury that surprised even herself.

"Casey, you can't —" Keith began, with a worried look on his face.

"I can so! Just try and stop me. If Mr. Kreevitch starts up that chain saw, he's going to have to saw *me* in half, too." She squeezed her eyes shut and pressed closer to the maple tree.

Mr. Kreevitch looked thoroughly puzzled. "Gosh, I don't think Ms. Allardyce is going to like this."

"I don't care. Go and get her, and we'll discuss it. I'll prove to her that — that this tree is a Canby Hall landmark. Yes, that's it! The tree has been here for generations of Canby Hall girls, and it means just as much to everyone as that silly old statue of the lioness."

"Casey, are you sure you're not asking for trouble?" Keith asked. "I mean, I'm a conservationist and all that, and I believe in traditions just as much as you do, but to get Ms. Allardyce mad at you is just plain suicide, isn't it?"

Casey's chin went up defiantly. "One has to have the courage of one's convictions, Keith." She had read that somewhere, at some point. And besides, she was no stranger to the power of protesting. Not after she and the others had succeeded in thwarting Owen Canby's plans to sell the Canby Hall property a few months ago.

"I'm not sure what I should do," Mr. Kreevitch said, turning to Keith. "I don't want to hurt the girl, but I have to do my job."

Keith tried to soothe the man. "Why don't you just go off and talk to the headmistress," he suggested. "She'll have a solution for this problem. And maybe by then Casey will have cooled off, and accepted the inevitable."

"Inevitable, my aunt Fanny!" Casey bellowed. "There is no reason why this perfectly healthy tree should have to die. If the electric company wants it trimmed, then let them trim it — but just a few branches. I am not going to allow the whole tree to be sacrificed."

"You may be sacrificing yourself, Case," said Keith, shaking his head with worry.

Ms. Allardyce, as it turned out, was nowhere to be found. But the majority of the girls in Baker House soon took up the battle cry with Casey, and within an hour, Casey Flint was the Canby Hall heroine of the day.

"Save our maple tree!" Shelley called out patriotically, hanging from a window because she wasn't allowed to leave the dorm. Faith, ready always with her camera, was on hand to snap dozens of photos of the drama that was unfolding at the base of the tree.

"If we have to, we'll chain ourselves to the tree," Ginny Weissberg told Casey. "But I don't think it'll be necessary. We have Mr. Kreevitch pretty buffaloed, for the moment. He won't try to do anything until he can talk to P.A."

"And where is P.A., anyway?" Cheryl Stern asked. "No one seems to know where she's gone to. It's not like her to go off without leaving some sort of message of her whereabouts."

"That's right." Faith focused in on Casey,

who was now perched like a wood sprite in one of the lower branches, and snapped another picture. "I went looking for Ms. Allardyce myself, to see if I could get a quote about the tree for the *Clarion*. There was no one at her house, not even her ever-faithful house-keeper."

"Her car, though, is in the garage," Ellie Bolton told them. She was handing out mugs of coffee and a platterful of doughnuts to all the demonstrators who had gathered around Casey.

Nobody mentioned, of course, the fact that Shelley had been driving P.A.'s car last night. It was a taboo subject, ever since Dana had warned them all to mind their own business.

"Casey, I think you're terrific," Ginny said, looking up with admiration at the girl in the tree. "We all do. Why, this dorm just wouldn't be the same without the old maple. And you're right about it being a landmark! This tree was here when my mother and grand-mother attended classes at Canby Hall."

"So if we have to, we'll call up all the alumnae," Casey said. She was thoroughly en-joying her position as acknowledged leader of this campaign. "They'll back us up. And Dana — have you notified any of the local newspapers yet? I figure they'll want to get the story and lots of photos."

Dana smiled, amused. She could see that Casey was playing her role to the hilt. Susan

B. Anthony couldn't have done better. "Not yet, Case. First we'll wait to see what P.A. has to say to us. I don't think we should embarrass her until we know just how stubborn she plans to be."

"That's right," Ellie Bolton agreed. "Maybe she'll see things our way."

Keith was looking up at Casey as though he'd lost his best playmate. "Are you going to stay up there all day, Casey?"

"Oh Keith, I'm sorry. But a woman's got to do what a woman's got to do." Casey paused a moment, for effect. "It's not easy, being a public figure like this."

"You're a true heroine of our decade, Casey," one of the girls called out.

"Thank you, sisters, thank you all." And Casey was grinning from ear to ear.

"How's it going, Shelley?" Faith said when she and Dana returned to Room 407 from the excitement outside.

"Awful. I'm starting to hate being grounded. All the rest of you are out there in the beautiful sunshine. . . ."

Dana put a hand on top of Shelley's curly blonde head. "Hey, kiddo, you know the solution. All you have to do is level with Alison. If, as you say, you have a good and legitimate reason for what happened."

Shelley laughed bitterly. "Sure. But I'd much rather tell her a big, whopping lie. Like a bunch of gangsters came at me with knives and guns, and before I knew it, I was driving them to the Greenleaf Bank for a heist."

Faith looked horrified. "That's not what happened, is it?"

"Oh, Faith." Dana didn't know the answers any more than Faith did, but she knew that that wasn't the story. "You haven't heard about any bank heist last night, have you?"

But even Dana began to frown and gave Shelley a sideways look, as though wondering if there was any truth at all in the mention of gangsters.

"Telephone for Shelley Hyde," called out Heather, knocking on the door to 407. "It's the phone on the landing down the hall, Shel."

"Thanks, Heather." Shelley hurried off.

"I don't know what to think of her anymore," Dana said. "Do you think it would help if we spied on her phone call?"

"Who knows? Maybe. But first, Dana, I've already done some spying of my own." Faith reached into Shelley's knitting bag and pulled out the small green wallet that Shelley always carried. "When she was out of the room before, I went snooping around. I know it was low of me, but she's in trouble, and I want to see what I can find out!"

"I understand. I'd have done exactly the same, if I had thought of it. So what did you find?"

"Look." Faith opened the wallet. There, sitting among Shelley's quarters and pennies and barrettes, was a set of car keys.

"Oh, no," Dana breathed. "Don't tell me they're — ?"

"They must be. They're for a Buick. And she's never carried car keys around before. But now. . . ."

Dana sat down, feeling actually sick with concern. "Why?" she said. "Why is our Shelley carrying those car keys in her wallet?"

"There's no point in asking her. She won't answer us."

"Okay. I still say we'd better keep a close eye on her. What if she plans on trying to use the car again? One of us should be with her at all times — do you agree, Faith?"

"Agreed. And what about your other suggestion? Why don't we follow her, right now, and see what her phone call is about."

"Maybe it's the gangsters calling," Dana complained, heading out the door. "Maybe they want her to be their hit man from now on."

Faith and Dana sneaked up on Shelley, tiptoeing through the double doors and finding a perch on the stairs. But they were disappointed to hear that she was only talking to Tom Stevenson.

"I'm sorry, Tom," Shelley was saying, and she sounded close to tears. "There's nothing I can do about it. We'll just have to postpone our date until some other night."

"We'll never learn anything from this conversation," Dana whispered to Faith. But they stayed huddled at the top of the stairs anyway, ears glued to Shelley's voice.

"I know, Tom, I know this is the last night for the play. And I was dying to see it myself. Look, as long as you've got the tickets — well, I suppose *you* might as well go. Couldn't you take your mother?"

Then Shelley made a horrible sound, like a wounded ostrich. "What do you mean, another girl? Elizabeth? Why would you want to go out with HER? Are you trying to make me jealous, Tom? Because if you are, I think you're terribly cruel. I can't help being grounded." After a pause, she continued. "No, I can't explain, even to you, why I was in the car last night."

"Poor Shelley," Faith said in a low voice. "Maybe we'd better get out of here, and leave her to her misery."

But just then the telephone receiver was slammed down with a fierce bang. Dana and Faith wondered how they were going to sneak away in a hurry, without Shelley seeing them. They began to slither along the floor, like snakes, backing up toward the doors.

They needn't have bothered.

"I know you're there, Sherlock and Watson," Shelley called out. "You're about as quiet as a herd of elephants."

"Oh. Sorry, Shel, but we thought we might be able to help in some way —"

"I know." Shelley sighed deeply. "I know you only want to help. But now I'm going to lose Tom, and nobody can help!"

CHAPTER TWELVE

I'll stay with Shel for a while," Faith whispered to Dana, "if you want to go back and rally with Casey at the tree."

But Dana didn't feel much in the mood for Save-the-Tree heroics this morning. She was worried about Shelley, she was sad for Faith and Johnny, and as for herself, she was wondering whether she could ever patch up her friendship with Terry.

She left the dorm and went to the library on an impulse. There she asked the girl at the desk about stories by Ray Bradbury.

"Oh, sure. He's very well known," the girl said. "If you want to read his stories, there's a whole section over there on science fiction."

A whole section. Dana was impressed. Science fiction was something that had escaped her notice all of her life, for some reason. She was a voracious reader, but had never cared much for thoughts of outer space or weird future societies. She hadn't even liked the movie *Star Wars*, when everyone else in the world had loved it.

Guess I am ignorant on this subject, she thought, as she made her way over to the sci-fi part of the library. Row after row of books, many by really well-known authors, caused her to rethink her stubborn position.

This definitely was a respectable genre in the literary world, Dana admitted now. And, as she leafed through some of the books with short stories in them, she saw evidence of many bleak, warning-type tales such as the one Terry had written.

Dana still didn't feel like reading any of it. Her tastes ran in other directions. But at least she saw what it was all about now. There would probably always be a market for sci-fi, she thought. There would always be people looking toward the future, and writers who could stretch their imaginations in a big way.

And at least she had an idea of what she could do now.

She headed toward the costume room, downstairs in the library, that belonged to the Drama Society.

Dana stationed herself outside of the boys' basement suite, knowing that Terry would soon be coming out for lunch; Keith had told her so.

When Terry did open the door, he was

greeted by a fearsome apparition. A tall, hairy creature that looked like Chewbacca the Wookie stood in the hall, unsmiling and unrecognizable.

"Okay, very cute," Terry said, laughing. "So somebody else is as crazy as me. Who is it? One of you town boys again, trying to pull tricks on us?"

Terry went over to get a closer look. "You sure are UGLY," he said cheerfully. Terry, being a professional prankster himself, always appreciated a good joke of any sort.

A deep, muffled voice came from inside the Wookie's head.

"I came to say that I'm beginning to understand science fiction now," it murmured.

The look on Terry's face was classic amazement. "*Dana?*"

"That's right. Dana here to say she's sorry, Commander." The voice was still totally disguised, as though she were talking through a wad of Kleenex tissues inside that head. Which she was.

"I don't believe it!"

"Believe it. I really am sorry."

"No. I didn't mean that. I mean, I never thought you were goofy enough to pull a neat stunt like this." Terry was smiling. "I am impressed."

"Well, do you think you want to forgive me? I was pretty ignorant, but I've done my homework now and — I've learned more about sci-fi."

Before Terry could answer, Faith appeared around the corner. "Don't anybody move!" she ordered. Her camera began clicking away, and she moved in closer to get some shots of the creature and Terry.

"Didn't mean to ruin your big scene, folks, but I'm getting a nice portfolio of pictures on this Truth Pledge experiment."

Terry was shaking his head. "You girls are crazy, do you know that? How did I ever end up at a school like this?"

"That's easy," Faith said, grinning. "Because you fit right in!"

Now Terry really laughed. "You're right, Faith. But sometimes I think you girls have got me beat by a mile."

The Wookie took the tissues out of her mouth.

"So? Do you forgive this interplanetary creature, or not?" she demanded.

"Of course I do." Now he looked slightly sheepish. "As a matter of fact, I'm the one who should be ashamed — and apologizing, Dana. You were just trying to be helpful, and that's what constructive criticism is all about."

"I didn't have to be so flippant and brutal."

"Nah, you had a right to your opinion. Feelings count, too, after all. And we forced you to give that opinion, against your will." Terry went over to hug the ugly Wookie in a friendly way. "No, I'm the one who should really be sorry, for being such a bonehead. *Childish*, Keith called me, and he was right!"

CHAPTER THIRTEEN

With all the excitement of the day — Dana's costume, and making up with Terry, and Casey's tree campaign — the girls from 407 completely forgot about Mrs. Merriweather — that is, until they had reached the dining hall in time for lunch.

"Don't forget, we have to bring back some food for Casey," Shelley said, as they stepped into the building. "Ugh. What can that smell be?"

"Smells vaguely Chinese," Faith guessed. "Could it be that our revered cook has concocted one of her chow mein specialties today?"

"One can only hope — not." Dana wrinkled her nose at the peculiar odor wafting through the hall. "You know, I've always loved real Chinese food, back home in New York, but what Canby Hall does to the stuff defies description."

"You can always drown it in soy sauce," Shelley suggested helpfully. "But then you'll be so thirsty that you'll — uh-oh."

"Uh-oh what?" Faith asked. Then she took a look, too. "Uh-oh is right. Here comes Mrs. Merriweather!"

"We're in for it now," Dana whispered. "We never planned what we were going to tell her. And we can't lie. We're still committed to the Truth Pledge. Oh please, floor, swallow us up."

There was no escape. Mrs. Merriweather came bouncing toward them with a big smile. She was dressed up for the occasion, with tightly wound curls in her white hair and even a touch of pink lipstick. Somehow that made it all the harder for the girls.

"Where shall we talk?" Mrs. Merriweather said without wasting any time. "And don't you worry, I've told the other cooks to save you plenty of chop suey, so you won't have to go hungry."

"Oh, goodie," Faith said with a straight face.

"How about right over there on that bench?" Dana suggested.

They all sat down, the girls with great discomfort, and Mrs. Merriweather with the air of going to a really great party.

"Okay now, out with it. What are your

feelings, girls? What is your evaluation of the food here at Canby Hall?"

There was complete silence.

"Well? You promised that you'd discuss my meals. You can't let me down now!"

"Um, you put out a wonderful salad bar," Faith ventured.

"And the morning coffee is usually, er — a real eye-opener," Shelley said. "Just what we need to wake us up."

"Nobody can make baked chicken like you can, Mrs. Merriweather," Dana hedged. (*Nobody else would* want *to*, is what she was really thinking.)

They knew that their answers were a cop-out, but Mrs. Merriweather began to beam, and her cheeks looked unusually rosy.

"So you really think my meals are all right then? I thought — well, some of the girls complain behind my back, but I often hear them. And then I get to feeling rather blue."

Faith, Dana, and Shelley fell into a guilty silence.

"But if you three think that the food is A-okay, why then, I guess it can't really be so bad, can it?" Never had the girls seen the cook with such a satisfied look on her round face.

Shelley took a deep breath. "I *have* to tell the truth. I mean, these are the Truth Pledge days, aren't they?"

Her friends stared at her in disbelief.

Shelley forged ahead bravely. "Mrs. Merriweather, we are among those who complain, too. In fact, we complain a lot."

Dana groaned. Faith hid her face behind her two hands.

"You do, Shelley?" Mrs. Merriweather looked confused.

"Yes, ma'am, we do. But I want to explain. It's because we're not really used to such — such strange sauces, and some of the meats that are UFOs — unidentified floating objects."

Dana saw, out of the corner of her eye, Pamela Young standing nearby, watching and gloating.

Shelley wasn't finished. "You know, Mrs. Merriweather, the thing is that most of us come from small families, and our mothers cook in different ways, geared for fewer people."

"Well, that certainly makes sense," the puzzled cook agreed. "I have to cook for hundreds here."

"That's my point," Shelley went on. "We understand, too, that you have a very limited budget. So, I guess what I want to say is this: We *really* think that you do the best you can, for having to stick to that budget and still feed such a horde of hungry kids."

"My goodness." Mrs. Merriweather sat perfectly still, with her hands folded in her lap. "I appreciate your honesty, Shelley. I really do. And I thank you."

Unobtrusively, Dana patted Shelley on the

back, as if to say, "Well done." They were proud of their friend for managing to combine manners and tact with honesty.

"You're okay, Shel," Faith whispered.

But Mrs. Merriweather wasn't about to adjourn the meeting yet. "I'll tell you what. If the sauces are that strange, and the meats so unidentifiable, maybe what I should do is take a poll among all the students. You know, ask them all what menus they'd like to see featured."

"What a great idea!" Dana said with enthusiasm.

"Yes. I'm sure the kitchen staff can try to plan out a few special treats that everyone would enjoy," the cook said. She stood up, suddenly full of energy and drive. "I'll get to work on it right away! Again, thank you, girls."

She marched off toward the kitchen, pleased with her plans.

"Well, that wasn't so bad after all," Dana breathed. "Thanks to you, Shelley."

"She's actually going to conduct a poll," Faith said. "I've got to get some photos of this! It's like history in the making here at Canby Hall."

"You know what?" Shelley flashed them a smile. "This whole thing might just result in some better food around here, for a change. I guess that proves that honesty really *is* the best policy."

"Or, truth is stranger than fiction!" added

Dana. "Wait until we tell Casey about this. We actually outsmarted Pamela and her dirty trick. I guess that will put Casey's mind at rest. There's nothing that Pamela can do to hurt any of us."

The chop suey was worse than anyone could have imagined, but the girls from 407 felt obliged to eat some of it, with Mrs. Merriweather watching them joyfully.

"No wonder the Chinese put up a Great Wall around their country," Faith said, taking a swig of water to wash down the rubbery bits of chicken in the entree. "They must have known that one day, in a land far away, a cook like Mrs. Merriweather would attempt to imitate chop suey — and produce something like this!"

"Too bad they didn't build their Great Wall higher," muttered Dana.

"Ssssh, don't let her hear you," Shelley said, throwing a smile toward Mrs. M. "It's not THAT bad. I even took extra — I have it wrapped up in a plastic bag to take to Casey."

"You actually *stole* some of this chop glooey?" Dana looked amazed. "Why, if you'd just asked Mrs. Merriweather for some extra, she would have provided you with enough for the whole Eastern seaboard."

Terry, sitting with the roommates, laughed at the idea of Shelley and her contraband bag of Chinese food.

"I don't know about you, Shel," Faith said,

shaking her head. "Stealing food now. It seems as though you *are* heading down the road toward a life of crime."

"No sweat," Terry told them, his face a mass of freckles and laughter. "Anyone who would get caught stealing food from *this* mess hall could easily get off — on a plea of insanity."

CHAPTER FOURTEEN

Up in the maple tree, Casey was leading a medley of songs, and her crowd of followers was singing along feverishly. At various times, some of the girls would circle around the tree, reciting the poem by Joyce Kilmer ending in, ". . . poems are made by fools like me, but only God can make a tree."

It was an exhilarated group. The beauty of it was, all of the girls really felt sincere in their love for the old maple. All of them had enjoyed sitting in its shade at one time or another, for study sessions or just plain goofing off. Many of them had sat in the lower branches, as Casey did now, just to watch a bird building a nest or a tiny caterpillar winding its way down the trunk.

"Save our tree! Save our tree!" the girls chanted every so often, especially if they thought they saw Mr. Kreevitch anywhere around. It was odd, they were all saying, that the headmistress hadn't showed up yet, but word had it that she was nowhere on campus.

"I wish P.A. would get back here," Casey said, her eyes gleaming with the excitement of The Cause. "Because I'd like to get in touch with the media, if this is going to turn into a battle against Canby Hall."

"She probably has a hot and heavy date," one of the girls suggested sarcastically. "After all, she's been missing since yesterday and that's pretty scandalous."

Just then the girls from 407 came around the corner, with Shelley carrying her little bag of food for Casey. Shelley wasn't allowed to be out, of course, but she thought she could bend the rules for just one minute, to deliver the lunch.

"I heard what you just said!" Shelley's face was flaming with some sort of anger that no one could understand.

"What? About P.A. having a hot date? Well, why not? It's possible that she has a love life, you know."

"You're making up things," Shelley retorted. "And back where I come from, that's nothing but malicious gossip. Slandering a person's good name. And the truth is, you don't even know the truth —" She stopped herself short, just before she said something that she shouldn't have.

"Hey," said Faith, putting out an arm to

steady Shelley. "Take it easy there. You look like you're about to explode!"

"Well, maybe I am. I don't see any reason for anybody to be slandering Ms. Allardyce, when she isn't here to defend herself. . . ."

"Since when have you ever cared about Ms. Allardyce?" Dana asked. "You always avoid her, Shel, and you know it."

None of them was aware that Michael Frank, the school psychologist, was standing nearby, behind the thick lilac bush, listening intently to this entire exchange. Michael was an intelligent and kindly young man, whom all the students liked. He was as puzzled as the others about Shelley's odd reaction to the gossip about the headmistress. He had heard about Shelley driving Ms. Allardyce's car and wondered if there could be a connection between the two incidents.

"Well, wherever P.A. is, I just wish she'd get back!" Casey repeated. "I'm getting exhausted, sitting up here in this tree." She looked at the bag of weird Chinese food. "Do I really have to eat that?"

At that point, Alison came marching toward the tree, looking up at Casey with a deeply pained expression on her face.

"Well, here comes part of the Administration," Faith said, and aimed her camera at the housemother.

"Alison," Casey cried out. "Why so glum,

chum? Surely you don't object to this demonstration, do you? You're always so cool. And you know that we have right on our side!"

"Sorry, but I need to talk with you, Casey," Alison said. "Come on down from there. It's turned into truth time for you."

Casey frowned, but she didn't budge out of the tree.

"Okay, have it your way." Alison put her hands on her hips and stared up at the nervous Casey. "Want me to speak to you in front of everyone?"

"Please do speak," Casey said, trying to look brave. "I have nothing to hide from my sister protesters — or anyone."

"That's not what Pamela Young says."

Now Casey seemed to turn a shade of khaki green. "I can't imagine what Pamela Young could say that would have anything to do with me," Casey stammered. At the edge of the crowd, she spotted Pamela's face, twisted into a satisfied smirk.

Alison stared at Casey until she had her full attention, eye to eye. Casey didn't try to look away.

"Pamela tells me that you have used this maple tree, on occasion, to sneak out of your dorm room, Casey. After hours."

"To sneak out —" Casey was blustering, as though the charge was absurd. She looked up toward her window, way up on the fourth floor, as if to point out, silently, what a difficult thing that would be to do. Who would be crazy enough to climb down that many branches?

"These are the Truth Pledge days, Casey. And you did sign the pledge." Alison was trying to be quite stern, although her heart wasn't really in this. She didn't like to force anyone to rat on herself.

"Is that true, Casey?" Ginny Weissberg and some of the other girls looked disappointed. "If you used the tree to sneak out at night, after curfew, then this protest is really not such a noble cause after all."

"Yeah, I don't think I want to be associated with it, if that's the case," added Ellie Bolton. "Is it true?"

Casey Flint went through all the torment that Pamela had intended for her to suffer. Should she tell the truth, or shouldn't she? She looked down at all the girls who had regarded her as a heroine, and who now would lose respect for her, if Pamela's accusation was believed.

She felt a tug on her foot. Someone was trying, quietly, to get her attention. It was Keith. Now where had he come from?

"Casey, whatever the truth is — tell it," he said softly. "You signed that pledge, and I know you want to do the right thing."

She looked at Keith. He was squinting because the sunlight was reflecting off his dusty glasses. He looked — oh, she had to face it — he looked like a nerd. But he was the darlingest nerd that Casey had ever known, and she loved him! And either way, she was going to disappoint him.

She sighed deeply. "Okay, Alison. You've got me. I will admit the truth."

"Which is?"

"That yes, I have used the tree once or twice. Well, maybe three or four times, but not more than that! I just shimmied down, after lights out, so I could take a little walk and get a little fresh air. It was no major crime."

"It's a major breaking of the rules, Casey," Alison reminded her. "And it changes things here quite a bit. This protest demonstration will have to come to a halt, right now."

"But — it can't! Mr. Kreevitch will saw down the tree! You can't make me give it up!"

Alison, tall and strong, reached out and pulled Casey off the branch. "You will have to cease and desist, young lady, at least until Ms. Allardyce returns. And I promise I'll ask Mr. Kreevitch to wait another day before he does anything with that chain saw." Alison looked regretful. "I happen to love the old maple, too."

Keith was smiling. "I'm proud of you, Casey. You did the right thing, telling the truth."

The heck I did! Casey protested inwardly.

"Well, well, I see the great tree demonstration is over," said the silky voice of Pamela Young, who was still standing on the edge of the crowd. She patted her blonde page boy into place whenever the wind threatened to move even one hair out of position. "And I guess Miss Casey Flint can just plan on spending her days on probation — along with that other chump, Shelley."

"I'll murder her!" Casey muttered. "I'll decapitate her!"

"You'll murder no one," Alison told her. "Now, let's get inside and discuss this over a cup of tea."

"What a bummer, Casey," Ginny Weissberg said. "I mean, we feel sorry for you and all, but this really does ruin the whole sacred thing about saving the tree. We're going to call it quits, too."

The rest of the girls seemed to agree, and the group began to wander away, grumbling as though they were totally disillusioned. All except Faith, who put a sympathetic arm around Casey's shoulder and led her away.

CHAPTER FIFTEEN

"So now we're both grounded," Shelley said cheerily.

A glum Casey had stopped by to visit in 407 after her talk with Alison. The four friends were sitting around on the mattresses having a little pow-wow.

"Pamela really did a number on all of us, didn't she?" Casey said. "I knew she would. And somehow, I knew she'd get me. But I never thought it would be so easy for her."

"Oh, sure." Faith spoke in her let's-face-it tone. "Pamela engineered everything. I'm sure she forced you to climb down that tree all those nights, right, Case? And she probably also arranged for Sheff to transfer here to this school, just to tempt me once in a while."

"In each case, she had to *tell*," Casey argued. "She had to tell the boys from town about the Truth Pledge, which made Johnny question you. And she had to tell Alison about me and the Tarzan act in the tree. . . ."

Faith shook her head in disagreement. "I still say, many of our problems really are problems that we created ourselves. We can't totally blame Pamela. So she opened her big mouth a few times. In my case, I was dangling Johnny along, not sure whether I liked Sheff a little bit, or not."

"Yeah, and you really *had* used the maple tree for your midnight strolls, Casey," Dana told her. "So it was just a case of your own sins catching up with you."

"And she told Alison about Shelley and the car," Faith added. "But Shelley really did drive the car, for whatever reasons of her own."

"I still hate Pamela," Casey said stubbornly.

"We all hate her; that's an established fact anyway," Dana said. "But there's not even a way to get back at her, not during Truth Pledge days."

"Oh no? I'll find a way," Casey vowed. "I'll find something she cares about a LOT — like maybe that boyfriend she's always bragging about, that Wilson Marchand III, out in California. And I'll —"

"You'll what?" Dana asked. "You can't tell any lies for these days, Casey. Come on, why should we let Pamela drive us crazy, when we could be having a good time instead?"

"Yeah? Doing what?"

"Playing something . . . Monopoly," Shelley suggested.

"Ugh, I hate that game." Casey made a face.

"Precisely why you should play," Dana said firmly. "It will get you so revolted that you won't have time to think about Pamela — or the wrath of P.A. So let's get started." Dana rummaged around in the overstuffed closet for the board game.

"Um . . . while you set up, I have to run one quick errand," Shelley said, rather mysteriously. Usually she expounded fully on what errands she had to do. This time she merely bolted out the door, calling, "I'll be back in a sec."

"Well," said Faith. "She certainly does share her problems with us, these days."

"Oh, why don't you stop worrying and roll the dice," Casey told her, getting into the spirit of the game now.

But Faith and Dana exchanged glances. They knew that one of them had to follow Shelley to see what she was up to. They had agreed never to leave her alone.

Downstairs, Shelley stepped nervously up to one of the telephones. Good. No one was around. Amazing for a Saturday!

She dialed the phone number of the Greenleaf Hospital.

"I'd like to speak to Ms. Patrice Allardyce, please, if it's possible," she whispered.

"What?" bellowed the switchboard woman. "I can't hear you!"

"I said. . . ." Shelley decided she couldn't whisper any longer. "I said, I'd like to talk to. . . ."

Just then Cheryl Stern came into the room, fishing through her jeans pockets for a quarter. She smiled at Shelley and stationed herself at a phone.

"Hello? Hello?" the hospital switchboard operator kept calling out. "Is there anyone on this line?"

"Yes. Never mind. I'll call a little later," Shelley said. She was frustrated and disappointed. This was the fourth time today she'd tried to call the hospital, just to see how Ms. Allardyce was doing, and maybe to talk to the headmistress herself, to send a note of cheer. But someone always wandered in. She couldn't possibly do it while there was anyone who could overhear. Shelley wandered out to the lounge, to wait until Cheryl had finished. But just as Cheryl hung up on her call, Faith came skulking into the telephone nook. She hadn't been able to locate Shelley yet, but she had a call of her own to make. Seeing no one around, she dialed Johnny Bates' number. Not that her life was any big secret, really, but she did hope for a bit of privacy for this call.

"Oh, Faith dear," Mrs. Bates said in a welcoming voice. "Johnny's not at home at all today. You know he usually helps out at the garage on Saturdays."

Faith had forgotten that. Johnny worked as many hours as he could at his father's service station.

"You can call him at the station, Faith," Mrs. Bates suggested. But Faith knew she wouldn't. There'd be too many men hanging around the garage, and Johnny would be teased for weeks if a girl called him with a lovelorn message.

So, feeling frustrated, Faith said good-bye to Mrs. Bates and hung up the phone. She'd just have to think of some other way to get in touch with Johnny. For now, she had to continue her search for Shelley. She decided to run over to Ms. Allardyce's house and look in the garage — just to be sure the Buick was still there. Who knew what Shelley was capable of doing these days?

Shelley waited until Faith had gone. Then she scooted back in and deposited another quarter. This time she was able to tell the operator who she wanted.

"I'm sorry, that patient isn't receiving any calls," the switchboard woman told her.

"Well, at least can you tell me how she's doing?" Shelley pleaded.

"I'm terribly sorry, but we're not allowed to give out that information to anyone."

"Okay, well, thank you, anyway." Shelley plunked down the receiver desolately. She was really worried about Ms. Allardyce. Suppose the headmistress was seriously ill, and Shelley was the only one at Canby Hall to know about it?

She also had a selfish motive in wanting to talk to Ms. Allardyce. If she found out that the patient was well enough, Shelley wanted to tell the headmistress that she'd gotten into all this trouble, here at school. She wanted to explain how she was grounded and couldn't even go out with her boyfriend, Tom. Then, maybe, Ms. Allardyce would explain things to Alison, at least.

Oh, well. If she couldn't reach the headmistress, she couldn't reach her. Shelley shrugged and started up the stairs, hating the dreary boredom of being grounded on a weekend.

Faith came in the front door, looking as though she'd been running. "Oh, there you are, Shel. Ready to go back to Monopoly?"

"Were you looking for me?"

Faith couldn't tell a lie. "Er — well, sort of —"

Shelley grimaced. She was beginning to get the impression that her roommates were keeping a close eye on her. And she thought that was rather comical — and very caring of them.

CHAPTER
SIXTEEN

The Monopoly game had no sooner gotten under way than Terry O'Shaughnessy knocked on the door of 407.

"Dana, can I see you for a moment?"

The other girls smiled. They were glad that Dana and Terry were friends again.

"You go ahead. I'll take your turns until you get back," Shelley offered.

Dana went out into the hall. "What's up, Terry?"

"Someone asked me to get you. He's downstairs in the lounge."

"Someone? A he?" Dana was perplexed. "Oh, is it Randy? Why would he be here in the afternoon?" She and Randy had a tentative movie date tonight, but she couldn't imagine why he'd show up now.

"No, not Randy," Terry whispered. "It's Keith. Says he needs to talk to you."

She went to the lounge. And there was Keith, all right. Looking like the Eighth Wonder of the World.

Keith was wearing the strangest — even for him — combination of clothes that Dana had ever seen. A huge, shiny, dark brown suit. A bright blue button-down shirt — well, that was okay, except that it was gigantic on him. And a tie that was impossibly ugly, with hundreds of green and mocha polka dots.

"Keith," Dana breathed. "Why in the world are you so . . . um . . . dressed up like that?"

Keith smiled proudly. "I found these clothes in my closet, Dana. I wanted to see what you thought of them. The suit and tie are from my Aunt Sadie. She likes to send me stuff that my cousin Barney outgrows. Will this do to take Casey out for her birthday?"

Terry was standing there, enjoying the scene. He said, "You gotta be truthful, Dana. Keith thinks he looks pretty spiffy in cousin Barney's suit and tie."

Dana gulped. She could just see Keith walking into some fancy restaurant, such as The Auberge, the French restaurant in Greenleaf, in that get-up. It was grotesquely unthinkable.

"Well . . . I don't think we've quite got it, Keith," she said kindly. "Why don't we just stick to our original plan of going to a men's store? Maybe we can even go right now, if I can somehow get out of the Monopoly game."

Dana shuddered again at the sight of that brown suit. "I'm sure we can find something that's much more — *you*. That outfit looks just too much like cousin Barney."

"But you don't even know my cousin Barney," Keith said, puzzled.

"Oh, yes," Dana said firmly. "I believe I do."

Terry was laughing so hard he could hardly talk. "If you want, I can go back up to 407 and tell them — what? No lies, now."

"Well, you can't tell Casey that I'm going to town with Keith, for heaven's sake! But you can certainly say that — that I needed to run into Greenleaf for a quick shopping trip. That's not a lie."

"You sure know how to stretch the truth, though, Dana," accused Terry good-naturedly. He went upstairs to relay her message, and Keith and Dana scooted out of Baker House before anyone could see them leaving together.

It was only a fifteen-minute walk to the center of Greenleaf and The Suitery, the nicest men's shop in town.

As soon as Keith and Dana entered the shop, a tall, balding salesclerk came hurrying over to them.

"Hi. We're here to outfit this young man," Dana said. "We're looking for a jacket and slacks. We were thinking of something in navy."

"Why, of course. Right this way, please." The fellow was looking at Keith as if he were someone from Mars, but that was all right.

"And what is the effect we're striving for?" asked the clerk. "Preppy? Business executive? Hmm, no, I imagine not. How about collegiate?"

"Just something dressy," Dana said. "For a special occasion with a special girl. And we want something that FITS."

The clerk eyed Keith's too-large brown pants with distaste. "Yes, I do see what you mean."

Keith was good-natured about everything. In fact, he began to enjoy making his selection from all the racks of nice, stylish clothing. He'd never taken time out to shop like this. He'd always been too busy with chess and mathematics and computers.

"This is kind of fun, Dana," he said as he came out of the dressing room for about the twelfth time. This time he was wearing just what Dana had ordered — a fabulous camel-colored jacket and the navy slacks with a sharp crease. The salesman had selected a shirt for him, and Dana had picked a tie that pulled the entire outfit together.

"Just take a look at that Dapper Dan in the mirror," Dana told him. "You won't believe that it's you!"

He stared for a minute at the unfamiliar, almost handsome person in the mirror. "This looks great, doesn't it?" he asked Dana.

"Absolutely." Dana smiled and made a circle with her thumb and forefinger to indicate perfection.

"You won't regret it," said the salesman, with a sigh of relief. "I presume you'll want to wear the — ah — new clothes now?"

"Oh, no," Keith said. "I have to save them for the birthday. No, I'll go home in my brown outfit."

"Oh." The salesman shuddered visibly. Dana couldn't blame him, but still she felt like giving him a right hook to the jaw.

"We have to get right back to Baker House," Dana told Keith. "I don't want Casey getting suspicious about us."

She literally had to drag him past the book shop. Apparently Keith couldn't pass a book store without wanting to go in and browse. "We can't," Dana said. "We have to hurry."

But when they passed a ladies' clothing shop, Keith would not be deterred. He went inside and told Dana to pick out a cardigan sweater, his treat.

"I'm so grateful to you, Dana, for helping me. I want to get you a gift."

"No, Keith, don't be silly. . . ."

"And not only that. I also wondered if you'd help me pick out a birthday present that Casey might like. One of those sweaters over there, maybe?"

Dana smiled at him. He was so cute and innocent. She grabbed a yellow sweater for herself, and much more carefully, selected a beautiful red silk blouse for Casey. She knew that

Casey, with her blonde hair, would look like a million dollars in it.

It was chilly when they went out, so Keith put on his jacket and Dana slipped into the new sweater.

They started walking back to Canby Hall, not aware that Pamela Young had been watching them in the shop. Pamela had made a complete about-face and gone quickly out to the street to hail a taxi. She beat them back to school, and had already visited Room 407 before they returned.

When Dana finally went back to the room, she found Faith and Shelley looking uncomfortable, and Casey staring daggers at her.

"So. You went out to talk to Terry, hmm?" Casey said. Her voice sounded dangerously devoid of emotion. Dana squirmed.

"You saw that I did. Why? Something wrong?"

"And then you went into Greenleaf. Alone, I suppose?"

"Casey, what are you getting at?"

"Oh, Dana, you'd better not evade the truth. It's Truth Pledge Day," Shelley cautioned. "And besides, Pamela was just here. Casey already knows. . . ."

"Knows what?" Dana tried to keep her cool.

"Knows that you actually went downstairs to be with Keith — not Terry!" Casey said, looking as though she was ready to cry.

"You went to town with *my boyfriend*, Dana Morrison. Just when I'm in the worst trouble of my life, you decide to steal Keith. Some friend you're turning out to be."

"Casey, you're getting hysterical over nothing. If a girl and a boy can't even have a conversation anymore —"

"Oh, but there's more to it than that. The whole thing is so sneaky, Dana. Having Terry call you out of the room so you can rendezvous with Keith. You've been really devious for the past two days. Tell me the truth — did Keith buy you that new sweater you're wearing? Pamela said he did."

"Oh Casey, how could you ever believe such a thing about Dana?" asked Shelley.

"Well? Did he?" Casey glared at Dana, her blue eyes like chipped ice.

Dana groaned. "I don't know how to explain this. Casey, yes, he did, but —"

"I should have been suspicious when I saw you having lunch with him the other day."

"Casey, you're jumping to conclusions," Dana said.

"I'm going to jump to a lot more than that!" Casey got up and marched out the door. "Maybe I'll jump off a cliff somewhere, one of these days. Then everybody will be rid of Casey Flint!"

"Casey, come back here!" Dana cried out, truly alarmed now.

"She's going to her room," Shelley said,

peering down the hallway. "I think one of us should go after her."

"Will you two do that?" Dana begged. "I'm going to get someone who can solve this mess, once and for all."

"Who?" asked Faith, as she took off toward Casey's room.

"The Best-Dressed Man of the Year."

Dana practically flew down the many flights of stairs to the boys' suite in the basement. *Please, Keith, be there,* she intoned, over and over, under her breath.

He was. He had just returned to the room and was still wearing the ludicrous brown suit and tie.

"Dana? What — ?"

"Come on, Buster," Dana said. "The birthday party is about to begin." She yanked him by his oversized collar and pulled him out of the room. "I'll explain on the way upstairs."

Terry looked up from the page he was writing. "Should I report this as a political kidnapping, or what?" he asked, laughing.

"You report anything," Dana threatened, "and I'll have to call you by an ugly name: *Pamela.*"

She marched Keith up those stairs toward Casey's room.

"Let us in, Casey, *please.*" Shelley was standing outside the door, knocking and pleading to no avail. "Please don't do anything you'll be sorry for. Dana's here now to explain everything. . . ."

"Go away," Casey croaked from within.

"She just won't open up," Shelley said. "But don't worry. Faith will be taking care of it."

"Where *is* Faith?"

"You'll see in a minute." Shelley went on with her coaxing. "Casey, please? There's someone else here to see you, too. . . ."

Before long the door opened, but it wasn't Casey who opened it. It was Faith.

"How did you get in there?" Dana was astounded.

Grinning, Faith said, "I climbed up the silly tree. I was scared out of my wits, but I did it — and then Casey had to let me in the window!"

Casey had retreated to a corner of the room and refused to look at the bunch who walked in. Dana spoke first.

"Now here's Keith, Casey. You've got to listen to his explanation, for heaven's sake."

"No," Casey said. She was all curled up in a ball and looked like a lost, forlorn child. "You want him, you can have him. You can —"

For the first time, Casey looked up. Out of the corner of her eye she saw what Keith was wearing. "Eeeeks. Why are you *dressed* like that?"

Keith stepped forward, smiling. "Happy birthday, Casey."

"What in holy heck are you talking about? I don't have a birthday! Not until . . . oh, well, next week, but. . . ." Casey seemed to have completely forgotten that her big day was so close.

"Happy birthday. I didn't want to spoil the surprise, Casey, but I guess I have to, now." Keith was shy and it was hard for him to talk in front of such a crowd of girls.

"What surprise? You're wearing a suit that makes you look like a Hershey bar . . . with a DISEASE."

"I know. I'm terrible about clothes. That's why I wanted to consult with Dana, so you wouldn't be ashamed of me, Case, when I take you to The Auberge for dinner on your birthday."

"You mean — that's what this is all about?"

Dana nodded. "We went shopping for clothes for Keith. And before we went, he was showing me some of his outfits, like this one, to see if any of them would be appropriate."

"Naturally she told him that this brown one was just the thing," Faith said with a straight face.

"Naturally." Casey started laughing, but then, suddenly, she began to cry. She tried to explain but all her sentences ran together.

"I can't believe it . . . I've been so awful to

you, Dana, and you were just . . . you were
being a fashion consultant . . . and Keith is so
sweet that he wants to. . . ." Now she was blub-
bering too much to continue.

"Well, that's one problem solved," Shelley
said with obvious relief as the roommates
went back to 407.

"Yeah. How is it that Dana always seems
to solve her Truth Pledge problems, these
days, when the rest of us can't?" Faith was
frowning.

"You just have to take the bull by the
horns, sometimes," Dana said, stretching out
across her bed. She looked exhausted. "In your
case, Faith, you've got to make contact with
Johnny . . . and tell him how you feel."

"Maybe you could write him a note, Faith,"
Shelley suggested. "You're always good at ex-
pressing your ideas on paper. Then, if someone happens to be going to town, they can
deliver it to him. . . ?"

"I'll try it," Faith said. "But who's going
to town tonight? Everybody, it seems, is
grounded."

"Or playing Monopoly with the prisoners,"
Dana added. "No, seriously, I'll take the note
to Johnny's house tonight. When Randy and
I go in for a movie."

So Faith began to construct a note. It wasn't
easy, and she tore up several sheets of note-
paper in the process. Finally she had it just
right.

CHAPTER SEVENTEEN

Hello, ladies. Someone told me that a psychologist might be needed here in Baker House."

Just as Faith finished her note, the girls were surprised to find Michael Frank, the school counselor, standing in the hall outside, knocking at their door. "Have there been any problems?" he asked.

"Oh, Michael," Shelley said. "There have been a million problems, it seems like! But we just solved one of them. Casey. She was afraid that Dana was trying to steal her boyfriend, and she —"

"She's all right now," Faith interrupted quickly, before Shelley got carried away. "Who notified you, Michael?"

"Someone phoned my house," Michael said. "May I come in, girls? I believe the caller was Pamela Young, although she didn't give her name. She wanted me to believe that Casey was suicidal, and needed expert psychiatric help."

"We're all about ready to murder that Pamela," Dana said. "Would you like to hear some of the things she's done to us, just in these two days of the Truth Pledge?"

"I certainly would." Michael looked around for a place to sit down, and then finally had to choose a mattress, one near the door.

"Hey, don't be nervous. I'm here as a friend," Michael assured them. "Really. I've been very interested in this Truth Pledge, but I didn't want to interfere at all, unless it was necessary. But now, from what I hear from Alison, all kinds of problems have been cropping up."

"Problems," Shelley repeated, becoming seriously theatrical. "You wouldn't believe —"

"Suppose you start with you, Shelley. You seem to be in the biggest trouble of all. What is this about the Buick, and the headmistress being missing?"

Shelley tightened her lips as though they were zippered. You had to give her credit, her roommates thought. She was as dramatic as an old Bette Davis movie.

"She can't talk," Faith interpreted for Michael.

Dana nodded. "That's right. She has this terrible secret that she won't tell to anyone. Believe me, we've tried to pry it out of her."

"Could she have some psychological trauma,

Michael?" Faith asked. "We've been wondering about amnesia, or temporary insanity, or . . . anything?"

Michael laughed, but he studied Shelley for a few seconds. He had a few ideas of his own. "She doesn't look at all worried, if you ask me." He sounded very professional in his evaluation.

"Which means?"

"Which means to me that maybe Shelley does have a plausible reason for what happened. So I guess we'll just wait and let time tell."

"But we have Faith's problem, still," Shelley said, breaking her silence at last. "Want to hear about that?"

Faith looked embarrassed. "I'd rather not talk about that, if you people don't mind. I think I may have it solved, as long as someone can take this letter into Greenleaf. . . ."

"I'm going into Greenleaf right now," Michael said. "Do you need an errand done? I'll deliver your letter."

"Oh, would you?" Faith looked at the clock; it was only about three o'clock. Not too late to catch Johnny at the garage. She sealed her letter into an envelope and wrote "Johnny Bates" on the front.

"Yes, I have to visit a friend at the hospital," Michael was saying. He was looking deliberately at Shelley as he said it.

Shelley almost jumped out of her skin.

"You're . . . you're going to the hospital?"

Shelley turned marshmallow-white, and looked like she wanted to ask more, but she didn't.

"Yep. Friend of mine has a broken arm from a tennis accident. I thought I'd go in and cheer him up."

"That's nice of you," Dana said.

Shelley was staring at Michael in a funny way. "Er, what floor is your friend on? I mean, I just wondered. Since we know so many of the nurses and people there now."

"I believe he's on the second floor," Michael answered, still watching Shelley intently.

Second floor. That was where they'd put Ms. Allardyce, Shelley thought. *What does Michael know?* she wondered frantically. But then, how could he know anything? Patrice Allardyce was telling no one about her hospital stay, and Shelley was certainly keeping the secret. Still, she had the uncomfortable feeling that Michael had guessed something, somehow.

"So I take this to Johnny Bates at the Bates Garage on Main Street," Michael said, repeating Faith's instructions. "And if he's not there, then I drop it off at his house, which is on Locust Street — correct?"

"Correct," Faith said. "And I really do thank you. You can't imagine how much this means to me."

Michael stood there at the door, poised to leave. "So . . . anyone have any other messages for me to deliver?" He was looking at

Shelley again. "Anyone at the hospital, for instance?"

"No, I can't think of anyone, can you?" Dana asked the other two.

Yes, Shelley was thinking. *Yes! Tell Ms. Allardyce to get me out of all this trouble, if she can. . . .* But of course she couldn't say any of that. She couldn't tell Michael a thing.

"Well, take it easy, girls. I'm sure that all your problems will turn out just fine, in the long run. And the Truth Pledge will be over by tomorrow morning. I imagine that Alison's cousin will have a very interesting paper to write for her psych class."

"Yes, and it'll be even more interesting if Casey finds a way to get even with Pamela," mumbled Faith after Michael left.

"Pamela deserves some sort of retribution," Dana said with a fierceness that was unusual for her. "She's gone entirely too far this time. Imagine calling the school counselor with a story like that! She's the lowest of the low."

Michael Frank drove slowly into town, reflecting along the way about Shelley Hyde. He had been doing some figuring, and had come to the conclusion that Shelley had reacted quite strongly to his mention of Greenleaf Hospital. He had also remembered her earlier at the maple tree, when she was fiercely defending Ms. Allardyce's reputation to the girls. He was putting two and two together, and he was beginning to think he had a count of four.

First Michael went to the Bates garage. He spotted young Johnny right away, waiting on customers at the gasoline pumps. Michael drove in to have his tank filled.

"Yes sir?" Johnny asked, when he finally was able to get over to Michael's car.

"I'd like you to fill 'er up," Michael said. "And I'd like to deliver a letter personally to Johnny Bates. Is that you?"

"Why, yes." Johnny looked puzzled, but then he smiled. "I think I know you. Aren't you the counselor from Canby Hall?"

"That's me. Michael Frank." The counselor smiled amiably. "And maybe you can also guess who this letter is from."

Johnny had been thinking about Faith a great deal, since last night. He was regretting the way he'd put her on the spot, using that Truth Pledge thing to question her about Sheff. He was also regretting the way he'd walked out on her when she tried to give him an honest answer.

"Thank you, sir," he said politely to Michael. He shoved the letter into his pocket, and went about his business, filling the tank with gas. He checked Michael's car for oil, and gave the windshields an extra-special cleaning.

"Do you want to read the letter, and see if there's a message for me to take back?" Michael asked.

"No sir, but thanks anyway. I'll just have to figure this out for myself."

When Michael had driven away, Johnny opened the letter. It smelled sweet and fragrant, just as Faith herself always did. She had written on a creamy, elegant stationery with light blue ink.

Dear Johnny,

I'm still under the Truth Pledge . . . and if the truth be told, there's a certain Greenleaf boy who has quietly had my heart for a long time now.

So I'm dazzled by glamor now and then — so what? We're all only human. I have realized once again that under all that sophistication, the jazz trumpeter is a pretty self-centered person, whereas the boy who has my love is warm and loyal and sweet.

If that certain Greenleaf boy can believe me, and forgive me, then I sure would like to treat him to a pizza tonight at Pizza Pete's. I am awaiting your reply.
Love, Faith

Michael Frank parked his car in the hospital parking lot and walked briskly into the building. He knew what room his friend was in, but he stopped anyway at the front reception desk.

On a hunch, he said, "I'd like to visit Ms.

Patrice Allardyce, if you can tell me her room number."

The clerk looked through her records. "Let me see. Yes. Room 233. But no visitors allowed, it says here."

"Oh, I see. Well, I won't bother her then, of course. I'll just visit with my other friend."

Michael headed straight for the elevators. So he had been correct after all, he thought. There had to have been something seriously wrong, for a good girl like Shelley to be driving Ms. Allardyce's car.

Instead of going to his friend's room, Michael went down the second floor hall to room 233. The door was partially closed. But he had come this far, and he wasn't going to let a door stop him. He knocked softly.

"Who is it?" The voice from inside was that of the headmistress.

"It's Michael Frank, Patrice. May I come in for just a minute?"

Silence. "I'm not having any visitors," she called out, frosty and furious. But then, "Oh, you might as well come in. I want to know how you found out about this, Michael!"

He entered the private room with a nice relaxed gait, smiling easily. "Come now, Patrice, what's all the secrecy about? I'm not going to ask you about your ailment. That would be an invasion of your privacy."

"Who," she asked precisely, "told you that I was here?" She was sitting up in bed, looking well rested and as well groomed as al-

ways, even in the hospital gown. Her hair
was neatly brushed back and pinned into its
usual chignon, and there was even a touch of
makeup on her face, to give her color. Yes,
she was the same old Patrice Allardyce that all
of Canby Hall knew and feared.

"It wasn't Shelley," he said without pre-
amble. "Actually, I guessed. The whole school
has been agog with rumors about your dis-
appearance, and I just made it my business to
keep my eye on poor little Shelley. . . ."

"Why do you say poor little Shelley?"

"Mmmm. This is going to be a long story.
Do you mind if I take a chair?" He hesitated
for a moment. "Are you well enough to talk,
or is this a bad time?"

"I'm well enough," she snapped impatiently. "In fact, I'm perfectly fine, as it
turns out, and I'm raring to get out of this
place. All my tests came back negative. At
first they thought it might be a heart attack,
but it wasn't."

"I see. I understand why you didn't want
the school staff to know. No administrator
likes to have it known that he or she could
be suffering from an ailing heart."

"Oh, stop playing the pyschologist, Michael.
Even though you're one hundred percent
right." She allowed herself to smile faintly.
"I felt it was nobody's business, if I was having a heart attack. That's why I pledged
Shelley to secrecy. But what were you saying
about her?"

"She's been having a rough time, Patrice."
Michael sat down and began to tell the story
as he knew it, and as Alison had explained
things to him. He finished with, "And the
biggest concern of the girl now is, that her
date with her boyfriend has been canceled because she's grounded. She says she's afraid
he'll ask some other girl to the theater."

Ms. Allardyce looked indignant. "Why, that
is a disgrace. Shelley was absolutely wonderful
to me when I needed help, and she certainly
does not deserve this! Of course, it's no one's
fault. Alison had no way of knowing what
was going on."

"Of course not," Michael agreed. "No one
did. And Shelley wouldn't say a word in her
own defense."

"She's a good girl," the headmistress pronounced, and put her head back on her pillow
rather tiredly. "She has wonderful manners,
and a very kind heart."

And that was very high praise indeed from
Ms. Allardyce. Michael was impressed.

Patrice Allardyce sat up with renewed vigor.
"Can you hand me that telephone, Michael?"
she requested. "I've got to settle this once and
for all for Shelley. I'll call Alison right now."

"That's just wonderful," Michael said. He
just hoped it wasn't too late for Shelley to re-
cover her theater date.

When all this is over, Michael thought, *I'm
going to have a talk with you, Patrice, about
a certain troubled girl named Pamela Young.*

CHAPTER EIGHTEEN

"Well, your letter to Johnny is on its way," Shelley told Faith. "Let's hope he'll call soon, and you'll have a pizza date for tonight."

"Ooops," said Dana. "*I* have a sort of date tonight, too. But we can't both go out, Faith. One of us has to be here for...." She pointed secretly toward Shelley. "I mean, maybe we can get Casey, but she might be with Keith...."

"And what's this all about?" Shelley demanded, although she already knew. "You think one of you has to keep an eye on me at all times?"

Neither Dana nor Faith answered.

"Hey, this is Truth Pledge Day, remember? You can't worm your way out of this one. Answer, my friends. Are you watching me as though I were a mental patient?"

"I wouldn't put it that way, Shel. . . ." Dana started.

"Not exactly that way," Faith said. And then she grinned. "But close!"

Shelley reached for her knitting bag, trying to look huffy. "For your information, I am not a mental patient. You heard Michael, and he's the trained psychologist. He thinks I'm perfectly okay. And so will you, once you know the truth."

"Well, we sure wish we knew it right now," Faith said. There was a knock at the door of 407. Before anyone could answer it, Alison let herself in.

"May I come in, gang?"

"Only if you bring happy tidings," Dana said wearily. "We can't take any more bad news, Alison. I'm sure you can understand."

Alison smiled. "This *is* good news, folks."

The three of them stared at her, afraid to breathe.

"Shelley, I just got a call from Ms. Allardyce."

Shelley's mouth fell open. She didn't dare say a word. She didn't want to give anything away, even now.

"The secret is out, Shelley."

"Is Ms. Allardyce okay? How is she doing? You really spoke to her?"

"She's absolutely fine. And she made it very plain to me that you are no longer to be grounded."

Before the words were out, Shelley shrieked with joy.

"You're kidding! You're not kidding? I'm off the hook? Oh wow, did Ms. Allardyce tell you the whole thing, Alison?"

"She certainly did, Shelley. I'm sorry about this whole mess."

"Hey! What's going on? What's this big secret that we don't know?" demanded Faith.

Shelley was practically dancing for joy.

"Oh, happy happy day. I mean *date!* I can call Tom and see if there's still hope for the theater thing. And if he asked Elizabeth or any other girl, I'll —"

"Sure, Shelley. You go and call him. I'll explain to Dana and Faith what the real story is."

Shelley flew to the telephone on the landing. She was able to reach Tom right away.

"Of course I still have the tickets, Shelley," he said. "Hey, this is great news! I'll be by to pick you up at seven."

"I'll be ready," said Shelley, and felt as though she were floating on air. All the pressures and tensions of the past day were leaving her. It had been awful, just awful, to be grounded and treated as a car thief. But that wonderful Ms. Allardyce had made things right again for her.

When she got back to Room 407, Casey was there, and all of them, even Alison, were celebrating the great turn of events with cans of diet soda.

"You're a real heroine, Shelley," Faith said.

"She certainly is," Alison agreed. "Not only did she get Patrice safely to the hospital, but she was able to keep that secret through thick and thin. And her problems really were thick!"

"And we thought you were — oh, Shelley, we're so sorry!" Dana gave her roommate a big, relieved hug.

"It's okay. Really," Shelley reassured them. "All is well with Tom — our date is on again! And I just want to say to you guys what I was starting to say before."

"What's that?" Faith looked a little wary.

"That you are the *greatest* roommates in the whole world. Imagine that both of you were willing to give up your Saturday night dates just to baby-sit me. . . . That shows me that you really care."

"Well, of course we care, you nut!" Dana stood with hands on hips, daring Shelley to argue with her.

"Thanks, pals. Like I said, you're the best friends on earth. And that includes you, too, Case. And Alison!"

"This is all so fantastic," Faith said, and reached for her camera. "Please, let me take a few pictures of this celebration."

"And now I have to inject a sour note amongst all this celebrating," Casey said, shrugging.

They all looked at her.

"Brace yourselves. It's dinner time at the dining hall."

They were a jubilant foursome as they crossed the campus green, heading for the dining hall.

"Even if she serves the chop suey left over from lunch, who cares?" Casey said. "This is a night for happiness."

"Yeah, but Casey, *you're* still grounded, and in trouble," Faith reminded her. "How can you be so high-spirited?"

"Oh, I'm happy because I have Keith back."

"You never lost him, Casey," Dana corrected her.

"Well, okay, maybe not, but in my mixed-up mind I had. And, best of all — I have a super surprise for one Pamela Young."

"This ought to be good," Faith said with trepidation. "You mean, you found out a way to get back at her? For all the rotten things she pulled? Even calling Michael Frank and telling him that you were suicidal?"

"Oh, did she do that, too?" Casey wasn't upset in the least. "Don't you worry, chums. Something unbelievable fell right into my lap a little while ago, and it's priceless! When I hit Pamela with this one, she'll be sorry she ever started on *us*."

"But, it won't violate the Truth Pledge, Casey, will it?" asked Dana worriedly.

"Not one iota."

* * *

They went into the dining hall, and were greeted by Mrs. Merriweather, sitting at a makeshift desk in the middle of the lobby.

"Hi, girls. This is the official menu poll. I'm talking to everyone in the school. I'd like you to tell me your favorite foods, so that I can —"

"Pizza."

"Pizza."

"Pizza."

"And one more pizza," finished Casey, after the roommates had spoken.

"My goodness," said Mrs. Merriweather. "That makes it almost unanimous. The whole student body has said the same thing, except for Pamela Young, who prefers beef Wellington."

"I'll give her a beef Wellington," said Casey smugly.

"So . . . pizza it is," the cook said. "I guess I'll just have my kitchen staff begin next week, experimenting and learning how to make it. I'm sure we can learn in no time at all!"

"That will be . . . uh . . . interesting," Dana said, and wondered if she had just violated the Truth Pledge irretrievably.

They went into the dining hall.

"Pizza," Faith said in a dull tone.

"Are you as terrified as I am?" Shelley asked.

"I certainly am." Dana grabbed for a tray as though in a state of shock.

"It's unthinkable," said Casey. "The Canby

Hall cooking staff, fiddling with something delectable like pizza."

"Ugh," Faith groaned. "Can you even imagine? They'll probably come up with Sicilian crust — but six inches thick!"

"It'll be covered with Polish kielbasa and sauerkraut," Shelley ventured.

"Dotted with Irish potatoes," added Dana.

"And cheese . . . don't forget the cheese," said Casey. "My guess would be . . . smelly old limberger cheese!"

Disheartened, the four friends moved down the food line toward the culinary surprise of the day. It was anybody's guess what the stuff was that was curdling away in the mystery gravy tonight.

"Why is that guy standing over there?" asked Shelley, after they'd been seated at their favorite round oak table. "The guy holding the long white box?"

They all turned their heads to look.

The delivery boy was asking directions of Mrs. Merriweather, who pointed to the table where the girls from 407 sat.

"Floral delivery for Miss Faith Thompson," the boy announced as he approached them.

"Floral. . . ?" Faith was too flabbergasted to move. Dana had to reach out and accept the smooth white box for her. And it was Casey who thought to pull some change out of her jeans pocket to give the boy a tip.

"Well, come on, Faith, open it!" Shelley urged.

"Flowers — for me?" She still looked dazed.

"If you don't open it, then I'm going to," Dana threatened. "And then *I'm* going to read the card before you do, and you'll be sorry. . . ."

"Oh, the card," murmured Faith, as though she'd never thought of such a thing. She carefully opened the box, and there was a bouquet of beautiful multicolored spring daisies.

"The card, dodo," Casey reminded her.

"The card — of course." Faith read it silently, and suddenly there were tears springing from beneath her thick dark eyelashes.

"I'll read it to you all," Faith said. "Because we've all been in partnership during this crazy Truth Pledge."

She read the note: "Truthfully, there's no one I'd rather share a pizza with. I'll pick you up at seven. Love, J."

"Where's your camera?" Shelley said. "Someone should take a picture of *you* now, with those flowers and that goofy look on your face!"

CHAPTER NINETEEN

So all's well that ends well," Dana was saying as the four friends stepped back into Baker House. Alison was standing there with her coat on, smiling at them.

"You all look happy," Alison commented. "And I have some more good news. Ms. Allardyce called again, and her doctor will release her from the hospital tomorrow. Michael and I will go to pick her up, however, Shelley. She's not worried anymore about people knowing her secret."

"That's great. And I'm so glad she's okay," Shelley said. "I was really worried about her for a while there."

"I'm sure you were. Michael and I are going to visit her right now. And Casey, I have some news for you, too."

"Oh, boy. Here it comes. Am I grounded for a year or am I expelled from Canby Hall?"

"Neither. I told Ms. Allardyce the whole story about the maple tree, and the confession you made yourself, in view of the Truth Pledge. She was upset, of course, that you broke curfew rules like that, but — believe it or not, she was in such a good mood that she said she wouldn't punish you. *This time*."

Casey's eyes opened wide with disbelief.

"You mean — I'm not grounded? I'm free? Out of trouble?"

"Yes. And as far as the maple tree goes, Ms. Allardyce said that she never thought of it as a Canby Hall landmark, but now that you've brought it to her attention, she agrees that it is. So the tree will be saved."

"Hooray!" the four girls yelled at once. They really did care about the tree, in spite of all the trouble that had resulted from Casey's campaign.

"But — those branches will be trimmed fiercely," Alison continued. "The power company insists on it. And I'm afraid all the branches near your window will be sacrificed, too, Casey. So you'll never climb out again."

Casey looked sheepish. "Oh well. I kind of expected something like that. It was too good to last, anyway."

"Hey, this is super," Faith said. "Now we're all free to go out tonight, and we all have a date. Should we go together? I mean, except for Shelley and Tom, who have theater tickets. We can make up for last night, when everything went wrong."

"Sure," everyone said.

"Everything went wrong," Casey said grimly, "because of Pamela. And now it's my turn to teach her a little lesson."

The girls waited in the lounge, knowing that Pamela would be coming across the green to Baker House momentarily. When she did walk in, she looked surprised — and then quickly bored — to see the roommates and Casey waiting there for her.

"Casey has a few things to tell you, Pamela," Faith said. Like the others, she was dying to know what it was.

An annoyed look flickered across Pamela's perfect face. "Nothing you four could say could possibly interest me," she proclaimed, wooshing right past them with her nose high in the air, in the grand tradition of the theater.

"Oh?" Casey was smiling with great satisfaction. "Not even some news about your friend Wilson Marchand the Third?"

Pamela stopped dead in her tracks. She tried to maintain her pose of complete and utter boredom, but it was obvious that she was dying of curiosity.

"I know I shouldn't ask, but just to make you happy, I will." She laughed, a merry little peal. They had all seen it done before, in one of Yvonne Young's movies.

"Remember, Casey," warned Dana. "The Truth Pledge. . . ?"

"No problem. There was a telephone call today for you, Pamela. Honest. No one knew just where you were, so I took the call." Casey was enjoying this. Her face was even more radiant than it had been this morning, up in the tree.

"A phone call for me," Pamela repeated. "And who was it?"

"It was old Willie . . . I mean, Wilson. The Third, of course. We talked for so long that we got to be real good pals, so that's why I started calling him Willie. . . ."

"Nobody calls Wilson *Willie*, Casey, so why don't you stop being obnoxious? You've got to stick to the truth, you know, or else you're going to ruin the good name of all Baker House." Pamela just loved holding the Truth Pledge over all of them.

"Oh, this is all the complete, unvarnished truth," Casey said. "I swear it. I called him Willie, and he called me . . . well, never mind that. The point is, I answered a few questions for him."

Pamela's face began to flush to a darker shade.

"*What questions?*"

"Oh. Well, here's what was happening." Casey stopped to flick an imaginary piece of lint off her sneaker. "It seems that Wilson was leaving California — right away, today, and heading for the East."

"He's coming here! Oh, that's the best news I've heard in a decade!" Pamela seemed truly excited. She'd been bragging about this golden-boy boyfriend, the cream of the crop, the last word in hunks and socialites, for quite some time now. "Now you people will see what a real boyfriend looks like."

"Mmmnn, I'm afraid not," Casey corrected her, shaking her head.

"What?"

"Well, you see, there were only three times that Willie could come here to Canby Hall. He's on a college-visiting junket, you see, and he'll be touring around the Northeast with his father. . . ."

"So?" Pamela was growing impatient with Casey's little games. But there wasn't much she could do to hurry her along.

"So, you can't reach him, of course, as he'll be on the road from now on. But he told me the three times that he could get here to visit you."

"And he'll take me out somewhere really ultraspecial," Pamela said dreamily. "No doubt we'll eat at the best restaurant in Boston. None of these Greenleaf restaurants will do for Wilson."

"Pamela, we ran into some snags." Casey tried to sound truly regretful. "Willie and I tried to work things out, but there just seemed to be no way. . . ."

"I don't understand. I can see him any time. What are you babbling about?"

"Well, here it is. The first time he could visit would be this coming Friday."

"That would be fine," Pamela said.

"Nope. I explained to him that there's a biology field trip that day. You know, to study the algae in the lake?"

"You dolt. I don't take biology!"

"Oh, Casey, did you tell a lie?" breathed Shelley.

"No. All I said was that there was a field trip. And there is." Casey put her hands in her back pockets and began to sing a little tune. It sounded something like, "Tie a yellow ribbon round the maple tree. . . ."

"All right. Very cute. So you got even for my telling about the tree," Pamela conceded. "But Casey . . . surely you knew that I'd be free the other two times that Wilson could come here?"

"Gosh. The next time he could come was the following Monday."

Wearily, Pamela asked, "You told him that was fine, didn't you?"

"Oh no. I told him you had a test to study for."

"What test? Are you crazy? What test?"

"Why, the President's Physical Fitness Test, of course. That's being given on Tuesday. I didn't lie. It really is on Tuesday."

"But nobody . . . nobody *studies* for a physical fitness test, you fool!"

"Well gee, I figured you would, Pamela," Casey said. "I mean, you're not in such great shape, you know."

Faith began to laugh, and Dana snickered. Shelley was trying to suppress giggles.

"This is not really humorous anymore," Pamela said dangerously.

"Neither were any of the things you did to us, Pamela," said Casey. "But you did them anyway, not caring who went to prison or got expelled or anything else."

Pamela looked like she wanted to turn and run, but she still had unfinished business. "Will you please — will you please tell me when Wilson *is* going to be visiting me?"

"Oh boy." Casey put on a long, sad face, but her friends knew it was completely rehearsed. "That's the hard part, Pamela. He said he could be here the very next Wednesday evening at nine o'clock. But — I had to tell him that there was no way you could see him then."

"You lied, then," Pamela howled, losing all control. "You lied, if you told him that, because I'm not going anywhere!"

"I didn't lie," Casey countered. "I'd never lie, during Truth Pledge days. I knew he was calling from California and so nine o'clock his time would be midnight here. That would be past curfew."

"Oh, you creep!" Pamela screamed. "That's not what he meant!" She was positively livid with rage.

"Oh really?" Casey said innocently. "So sorry, Pamela." And with that, Casey sauntered off, looking terribly pleased with herself.

CHAPTER TWENTY

Alison's cousin Maura was at Baker House bright and early on Sunday morning. Alison poured a cup of coffee for each of them from the huge coffee urn that Alison kept in the lounge for her dorm's traditional Sunday brunch.

"So. How do you think it went, Alison?" Maura asked.

Alison laughed and took a sip of her coffee as though she needed it for strength. "It was wild. We ran into more problems and more mix-ups than I ever dreamed possible."

"So you don't think the experiment went too well?" Maura looked worried.

"I didn't say that. On the contrary, I think the kids of this dorm were absolutely wonderful, coping with whatever came along. Michael was saying the same thing last night.

He was quite impressed with the resourcefulness of these students."

"Michael, hmm?" Maura smiled mischievously as she drank her coffee, and helped herself to a doughnut from the plateful on the buffet table. "Is he the man you're — um, dating? The one who's becoming pretty special to you?"

Alison laughed. "Why, Maura, are you planning to write another paper? The Family Grapevine Newsletter, maybe?"

"Well, you must realize that everyone in our family cares about you, Allie. They'd certainly like to know if anything serious is on the horizon."

"I'll tell you what. When there *is* something serious to write home about," Alison said, "then you'll be the first one I'll write to." And she settled herself comfortably on the lounge couch, putting her sandaled feet up on the beat-up old hassock.

Just then the girls of 407 came clattering down the stairs.

"Hope we're not too late for doughnuts and bagels," Faith was saying. "Oh, Maura — hi. You're here already."

"Hi yourself." Maura motioned for them all to have some brunch. "I'm awfully eager to hear from each of you about how the Truth Pledge went. Of course I'll be talking to each individual privately, but maybe you can tell me in brief — was the Truth Pledge a difficult thing for you all?"

The three girls poured their coffee and sat down with Alison and Maura. "Who wants to speak first?" Dana asked. "How about you, Faith?"

"Well, it was rough at times, yes," Faith confided. "But I got something really wonderful out of the Truth Pledge — a terrific batch of photos and a story that I can use for the school newspaper. So I can't complain!"

"I think we all learned a lot of things about ourselves," Shelley reflected, after swallowing a big bite of a strawberry jelly doughnut. "I remember when we signed up, we were bragging that we were completely honest people."

"And you found out otherwise?" prompted Maura.

Dana spoke next. "We found out that truth is a strange thing. What it boils down to is, we've learned that we *do* tell little white lies, just as Pamela said. We were shocked to find that out about ourselves."

Faith spoke next. "But maybe the white lies make us better people, because we try to be tactful in a lot of situations. We're trying, at least, not to hurt the feelings of good folks."

"Interesting." Maura raised her eyebrows.

"But," Shelley added, "we also found out that at times honesty is the best policy. Like with Mrs. Merriweather, the cook. We just couldn't pretend that her meals were hunky-dory when they weren't! So we should tell the truth when it's important, and not just say what the other person wants to hear."

"Well anyway," Faith concluded, "we tried to do our very best with the Truth Pledge. Even Casey, and she was scared to death of the whole thing. So I guess the experiment showed us that we do have a tendency to whitewash the truth, now and then."

"This is going to make a fascinating paper," Maura said. "I can't wait to hear each person's private story."

The boys from downstairs arrived just about then, tiptoeing quietly toward the doughnuts so they wouldn't interrupt the conversation that was in progress in the lounge. And Casey had arrived, looking bleary-eyed but eager to tell her Truth Pledge story.

"Mine will be the weirdest story on record," Casey admitted. "I was afraid to sign up because I thought that if I got into any trouble, Keith would lose respect for me. Because he's so honest and straight, and all." She blushed a little bit. "That's why I was so terrified of Pamela and what she might do. I didn't want to lose Keith!

"But what I learned was that Keith had *more* respect for me when I told the truth. It didn't matter to him what trouble I was in. He just wanted an up-front girl, someone with integrity."

She and Keith exchanged glances of real warmth and caring.

"So that's that for the Baker House confessions," Terry said. "And all I can say is this — I'm glad the Truth Pledge is now over. I mean, I feel like running all over campus and telling giant lies, just to celebrate!"

The others laughed.

"And I'll say one more thing." Dana stretched out her long legs. "The next time you have a psych experiment, Maura, would you please do one of those studies where they research the causes of ulcers in baboons, instead? Because we know the perfect volunteer to irritate the baboons. . . ."

"*Pamela Young!*" the rest of the crowd cried out in unison.